I AM ELIJAH THRUSH

James Purdy

I Am
Elijah Thrush

1972   Doubleday & Company, Inc., Garden City, New York

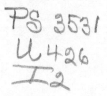

DESIGN BY RAYMOND DAVIDSON

Library of Congress Catalog Card Number 76–180099
Copyright © 1972 by James Purdy
Copyright © 1971 by Esquire, Inc.
All Rights Reserved
Printed in the United States of America
First Edition

For
Murray McCain, Paula Fox, and Forrest Frazier

I AM ELIJAH THRUSH

$\mathcal{M}$illicent De Frayne, who was young in 1913, the sole possessor of an immense oil fortune, languished of an incurable ailment, her willful, hopeless love for Elijah Thrush, "the mime, poet, painter of art nouveau," who, after ruining the lives of countless men and women, was finally himself in love, "incorrectly, if not indecently," with his great-grandson.

Because of my dependence on my habit, I was fool enough to become a paid memoirist to Millicent De Frayne, and because I am also black I was specially prized by her likewise on the ground many doors in New York would be opened to me which were closed to a white man.

My work was painful, as eating éclairs and napoleons seven hours a day might be, but my habit (which I will describe considerably later on) demanded I support it. Although my constitution is hardy, my nerves are delicate, and I had never been adept either at crime or at gainful daily employment. Nor was I gifted as a defender of my own people, although I live now and will, I suppose, continue to live at the Father Divine Fairgroves Hotel.

At the risk of leading the reader to think this story is about myself, let me say that I admire the violence and insurgency of my present-day "brothers" (a word I grin at nonetheless), but I can only live and be what I am, a desperate man, but a comfortable one. Perhaps, if I were lighter—Elijah Thrush on my first visit to the Arcturus Gardens, his studio, said bluntly: "You are the color of ripe eggplant!"—I might pass. My sole passion is my habit, and my task here is to earn for that habit by reciting the exploits of Elijah, as dictated by his "paramour" Millicent De Frayne. This story, neither in vocabulary or meaning, will be in the taste of the present epoch, and for this reason as well as others I embrace it wholeheartedly.

Because I am black everything is forgiven me by whites, and so this again may be the reason I have been entrusted with a story a white writer, straining for nobility, for current coin, would not dare stoop to pick up. I am allowed to be as low as possible, and there is always an apology waiting. Except from Millicent De Frayne.

She had no love of the human race, let alone the black, and her only interest in life seemed to be that I carried out her wishes. My kind of consistent, lethargic undynamic desperation made me "do." She was a direct woman and was forthright in expressing her surprise that I did not "smell." I think she was disappointed. She would have been more collected with me had I done so. Later on, Elijah Thrush corrected her indirectly when after having kissed me in a purely ceremonious way, he said, "Albert, you smell like a nocturnal moth I once crushed against my chest many years gone past, in Nebraska."

As the struggle to support my habit tires me greatly I was glad for the time to be in the company of such superannuated persons as Elijah and Millicent. They rested me, and all I had to do was listen and feign attention.

Attention gradually came, if not interest. And of course I wrote down what they told me. Yes, as close as it was possible for anybody to interest me, these two "unreal" old parties came near doing the trick. As the square world would have found them beyond the pale, I found them almost up to suiting me to a T.

"I am a difficult, I am an impossible woman," Millicent had begun that stifling hot July day, as we sat in her Fifth Avenue apartment. She did not allow air conditioning to be installed, and she kept the windows closed. As if to increase my discomfort, she wore a fur about her throat, which she occasionally brought higher about her neck, as if she was feeling a draft of arctic air.

"I have never worked with a person of your complexion," she began as she studied my necktie. "Frankly, you are not what I would have selected, had I the power of selection. But I am desperate. All the other memoirists have failed. They were miserable things, impostors all. I will not say I am counting on you, mind you. No such thing. But I have a kind of frayed hope. There is something about you that almost kindles optimism. Not quite. If you don't work out, have no fear. You'll be paid generously just as if you finished the memoirs . . . Now as to your duties . . . I want you first of all to listen to me. I'll go over his life with you, and you'll write down a skeleton of the facts. Then I'd have you go and *spy* on him. That's right, spy on him. Find out who his friends are, who he's seeing, and what's up with the child he calls the Bird of Heaven, who is his great-grandson . . . This is our bone of contention. I don't want him to love the boy . . . But first of all you must get to know the Arcturus Gardens, his dance studio and theater . . . I've kept him over thirty years in it, you understand."

"Have a dish of tea with me," Millicent then changed to

a voice of peevish command, and a gawky rawboned Swedish woman brought in a gleaming tea service. "We have only lemon," Millicent explained as Norah handed me a paper-thin exquisite cup adorned with forget-me-nots.

"I daresay I am the only person who is anybody who is not at the shore," she consulted a huge calendar on the wall. "Now I don't suppose you are afraid of bad neighborhoods, if you are, speak up at once, and I will hire a bodyguard for you. Good, you have no fear. I raise the question of mayhem at this time because Thrush lives in the district on Manhattan island around lower Tenth Avenue, which I understand in the days of good professional criminals they called Hell's Kitchen. The whole city should be renamed that today with good reason, for there's nobody among the living worth reckoning with.

"Now as to strategy!" she cried while she commanded Norah to pour me another cup of tea. Drops of perspiration were standing out on my brow, and I could feel Norah's interest, repulsion, and wonderment as she poured me more of the lovely gunpowder. "Wipe his face with a napkin, then, can't you?" Millicent told the maid. "He's dripping wet from the torrid day, though he comes, as you've noticed by his face, from where people are sunworshippers. Well, we all notice heat more or less, there's no gainsaying that, whoever we are . . . Now as to your task. You say you're not afraid of thugs, well and good. You're to go then to the Arcturus Gardens, where his studio is. Take this forged letter, though he'll know I wrote it or had it written. It's a request to have your portrait done. That's the smartest way to get into his studio." I put the letter in my jacket breast pocket. "He does portraits for pocket money, for his dancing recitals are canceled during the hot months, and even in the winter, they bring in hardly a thin dime in a month of

Sundays. Now, Albert—do you have a last name, by the by?"

"Peggs," I told her.

"P as in *porker?*"

I nodded.

"Well, Albert Peggs, you will go there, and of course spend as much time with him as you can stand to. Again, like heat, 'tis a matter of temperament. Many a person I've sent there couldn't take it and got deathly ill. He's not a health ad, you see, and hasn't washed his face in over twenty-five years because he feels it ruins the complexion. That won't bother you, though, will it? If so, say so. But be warned, the studio, though not as aired out as here, is *too* interesting: it recalls a zoo and an emporium of antiques, both, and, again like hot weather, is hard on the arteries. He'll ply you with questions because he'll know you come from me. I would simply decline to discuss me, if you don't mind. When he vilifies me, just smile, or do nothing, or agree . . . Where are those Scotch cookies I asked for, Norah?" she turned to the Swedish maid who was waiting, I gathered, to wipe my forehead again. "Well, fetch them before Albert goes off on his peeping-tom assignment, and whilst you're at it, my love, make him up a little brace of chicken dainty sandwiches so he can tide himself over till nightfall.

"Now Albert, my dear. I'll be frank with you about another matter also. In no way be too *intimate* with the Mime. I hope my warning is clear. I mean, you must not go over to his side. I'm the one paying the piper, and 'twon't do *a*-tall for you to take his part, or soldier for him. He's an abominable low mountebank when he feels the urge, which is most of the time, remember. But I've sent people before who've fallen in love with him. He is first-water mesmerism, no question about it, and in Old

Salem would have been burned at the stake. He is a wizard. I've carried the cross of caring for him, and have been only rejected for my pains. As I told you, or did I? he hates me to within an inch of my life, once told me he could eat my kidneys roasted on an andiron, and so on. But it's of me he thinks constantly, you see—obsessed with me, that is, and as I've loved him since 1913, this has to be my only reward from that quarter.

"How many sandwiches did you put in, Norah?" she cried as she took the ivory lunch box from the Swedish maid, and peeked into it. "Mmm, well that ought to stay him. Are you an awful big eater, Albert? Speak up, it's no crime if you have capacity. I won't let you suffer hunger pangs . . . Now, then, off with you to the Arcturus Gardens, or Hell's Kitchen or whatever, and be back here bright and early at nine tomorrow, and we'll begin our chores and chronicles in earnest."

"One last word of warning," she got out with great difficulty, refusing to take my hand, and leaning on a cane whose head seemed to be encrusted with jewels which blinked. "Beware of the piano player."

I nodded to let her know I would, but this irritated her.

"Don't ever pretend knowledge you don't have, Albert Peggs," she scolded. "You don't know him. He's incredibly wicked, and incredibly charming. Looks like those kewpies on merry-go-rounds, I always thought, so well groomed and clean, but a loathsome creature. He's shamelessly devoted to the Mime, and tries to prevent my ever communicating with him."

She suddenly took my hand in so convulsive a grasp that she clawed me painfully as she stuck, I thought, something in my palm and then, with a grip like that of a strong man, closed my hand tight.

In the street I noticed I was holding, in addition to the
forged letter in my jacket pocket, the chicken dainty
sandwiches in my left hand, no less than two hundred-
dollar bills in my right hand, which had now come open.
I stopped and blinked into the strong sunlight, for when
I had left her apartment I had made the vow never to
return, and of course never go near the Arcturus Gardens,
Hell's Kitchen (which I thought didn't exist), and certainly never see Elijah Thrush, formerly "the most beautiful man in the world." But there is no talking back to
two hundred-dollar bills, when you are the color of ripe
eggplant and sweat more easily than white quality.

I decided, despite the heat, to walk all the way to his
studio.

I arrived at last at the entrance to the Gardens, got
myself together, tied my tie though it was so soaked
with perspiration from my long walk from uptown
that it resembled a wilted poppy, and, raising my chin to
the right level of confidence without the angry hauteur
of my people today, rang the bell. A kind of tinkle
of dromedary bells sounded. Many bolts and locks were
heard moving, and the huge green door was pulled open,
and there with folded arms stood the piano player, Eugene
Belamy, about whom Millicent had warned me, daring
me to speak, double-daring me to enter. Despite his attempt to be formidable he resembled more one of those
toy bridegrooms on Italian wedding cakes than a real
watchdog, and, as I was later to understand, the cupid-
bow expression of his mouth was copied from the Mime,
his master, but unlike the Mime's was not formed arti-
ficially by Dorin lip-rouge.

"I am the bearer of this letter of introduction to Mr.
Elijah Thrush, the noted Mime and portrait painter," I
began.

"The evenings are closed now at the studio, I would have you know," Belamy intoned and began closing the door, but the thought of suddenly losing any future installments of hundred-dollar bills not only gave me the gall I needed here, but allowed me to walk immediately inside the room.

"I am sorry to be so forward," I raised my voice and looked him to within an inch of the eye, and shot out my chest, which is still despite my own advanced years (I am twenty-nine) something which frightens most white people, and my biceps have been compared in their best time to billiard balls. I am in short though ruined in all other ways still in possession of a perfect African physique. "And furthermore, what I have to say to the Mime will not wait."

"Where did you get it into your head (I think he was about to say *thick* but thought better of it), where did the notion come to you to address Mr. Thrush as the Mime . . ."

"I will not state my business to an intermediary, and I immediately demand to be given a seat and to be announced," I told the piano player.

"Well spoken, and beautifully delivered!" a somewhat cavernous voice came reverberating through the huge room into which I had walked uninvited. The bead curtains had parted, and a personage entered, whom at first I had mistaken for one of the accessories or paraphernalia of my own hidden life, for though I cannot grow pale, I can look ashen and unwell, and the personage standing before me, who was of course Elijah Thrush, seeing my altered state, immediately ordered the piano player to fetch his palm straw fan, and sitting beside me on a little hand-carved stool, the same deep voice began, "Call me mime if you will, for in all my years as an artist I have never set eyes on one with so primitively princely a presence as yourself . . . Will you retire to the recitation room, if you please, my dear Belamy," he addressed the piano player, who smirked a bit, but avoided looking at me, and left.

"Pray what brings you here when, as you heard, the evenings are closed . . ."

"I have come from quite a distance . . . Alabama," I faltered.

"You have no more come from Alabama than I have," Elijah Thrush said. "Understand my meaning," he tapped my knee at a bubble of contradictions from me. "You have come from destiny. You were meant to know me. I was meant to know you. Thousands of years ago we knew one another, you and I. And long after we have cast off the flesh and bones of this unworthy existence under which we suffer now, you and I will know one another again. I knew immediately I heard your voice you were the new person in my life."

I now gazed with less immediate dizziness at the face before me, though as it spoke I had the feeling a painting rather than a person was uttering sounds. There seemed to be no bone structure, indeed no skin, for what uttered the words was a kind of swimming agglutination of mascara, rouge, green tinting, black teeth, and hair like the plumage in a deserted crow's nest.

"Alabama indeed," he continued to fan my face. "You have come in response to the advertisement I placed in the newspaper of course," he whispered and now rose, and stood by a large concert grand piano.

"I have come," I began, falling now as I was to later, into his own language, "I have come only to know you, Mr. Thrush."

"Elijah," he corrected, and I saw now he was standing

that his body looked more substantial than his face, despite the fact that he had on a costume so lavish and fantastic that it, like the face above it, seemed to belong only to a picture.

"Everything you say goes directly to my heart," Elijah Thrush muttered and now began swaying and lifting his feet ever so slightly, so that I could see indeed he was a dancer.

Rising at last, I proffered him the letter of Millicent De Frayne, saying only, "This is my introduction."

Like the sudden change of weather in the open country, when the sun is almost in a moment blotted out by an unforeseen cloud, and both rain and hail beat on the unprepared traveler, his face was in a trice contorted with heavy lines, which gave it more the effect of flesh, but which would have frightened I am sure anybody but myself, and roaring as if I had knifed him, he cried, "You damned hired deceiver! You come from that rotten scum of woman! Don't defend yourself. Rise, and get out. Do you hear, get out! and vanish forever from my life!"

The beaded curtains parted and the piano player now came forward but more frightened than authoritative, while Elijah began tearing up the letter of introduction from Millicent De Frayne. "Go at once, handsome hireling, or I will summon the authorities."

But pushing the piano player out of the room, I went over to Elijah Thrush, took the last shreds of paper from his hand, handed them back to him, the larger portion of them at any rate, and said quietly:

"I have come to stay, Elijah. What does it matter who introduced us. We have met, and I am yours. Command me anything, but never to go out of your life."

"Are you, in God's name, real?" he exclaimed as he

began weeping, though I supposed then (but not now)
that this was play-acting.

"Look at me," he said, "and explain that you are real.
Comfort me."

Although white men had offered me their lust before,
nobody white had ever offered me illusion, together with
dream courtesy, attention, and the entire backdrop of
play-acting which was now poured out upon me. For a
moment I felt I would give up my attachment to my
expensive habit which had propelled me into the world
of Elijah Thrush and Millicent De Frayne in the first place,
and be only his, and yes perhaps *her* captive. But would
white kindness of even this insubstantial kind last? Wouldn't
it be followed as always by deceit and betrayal and en-
slavement?

"Do you realize what it is to have someone plotting
against you every minute of the day?" Elijah was speaking
of the "depraved" Millicent De Frayne. "Look at that
clock. You've heard it tick forty-two times as I point,
and in every one of those forty-two beats, she has thought
of forty-two ways to beat me to my knees."

Whether it was me, my past life, my race, whatever,
I found everything he said believable, and once my eyes
were accustomed to the sight of him, I found him, yes,
and here I thought my madness begins, I thought him
beautiful. I did not reject his caresses, and he went
on all this time indeed fanning me with the palm leaf
fan. It was a wonderful sensation. Occasionally I would
catch glimpses of the distorted face of the piano player
as he looked out at us from the beaded curtain.

"Pay no mind to Eugene Belamy. He is harmless. He
spits like a cat, but like a good tabby, he is soon purring
again . . ." Raising his voice, he scolded, "Eugene, you
should be practicing *The Cornish Rhapsody*. The last time

you played it was as rotten as I've ever heard it, and I've
had ten piano players to ruin it. I want perfection, damn
it, and what do I get but a mooning lovesick calf rendi-
tion à la Belamy.

"Alabama must be a particularly fortunate state if you
came from out of its depths," Elijah Thrush assumed
his conversational tone again, and as he fanned now so
close, from the inner recesses of my clothing a large
brown feather rose, like something alive, so that he caught
it easily with his hand. He put down his fan.

"Where on the face of the earth did this come from?"
he cried in a voice of superstitious awe.

"Belamy?" he began to call, afraid, then looking closely
at me, thought better of enlisting the aid of the pianist.
Meanwhile I was shaken with a fit of trembling. He kept
staring at me with his wild Indian-like pupils. "What is
the meaning of this feather?" he demanded. "Have you
brought it here and if so for what purpose . . . You
know what I am talking about, don't you?"

"In Alabama the unusual is the usual," I spoke out of
a mouth as dry as the time I had been held by the police
under a blinding bulb.

Elijah Thrush broke into a charming laugh, such as I
would imagine Cupid would give.

"It is impossible to be angry with anybody as fetching
as you . . . Yet God knows what you are up to . . . I
have never forgiven anybody as many times as I have
forgiven you, and we've known one another for only a
few minutes. You come from the one woman who has
done her level best to destroy me, you insult my piano
player and beat your way unannounced into my presence,
you show no knowledge of my genius or who I am,
you give me a forged letter, and then as I am fanning

you like your slave, the feather of a bird of prey falls out from your rich mahogany chest!"

Despite the humor of his queer phraseology, at his last words I became very agitated again, a kind of foam came from my lips, as I twisted about in the chair under his fierce scrutiny, and I had then to allow Belamy and him to lead me into one of the other rooms, where they removed my clothing, and began applying copious applications of witch hazel, but once I was bare they were both taken aback at, in Elijah's word, the display of jewels which I carried on my naked person. It was true, I had several bracelets, near my biceps, three necklaces, and a huge protective stone which I wear in my navel, but as I had lived with persons who thought these adornments "routine" I had forgotten what joy they give uninitiated people, even those so unusual as Elijah and perhaps even Belamy. The jewels convinced Elijah that I was beyond any peradventure of a doubt the most remarkable adult male of whatever color he had met.

"I do not say of *any* person because there is the Bird of Heaven . . ."

"I wish you wouldn't use that term!" I cried, a kind of raving anger coming over me again, and more froth poured from my lips.

"I beg your pardon," he spoke to Belamy, instead of me, as if Belamy had been the one to speak so disrespectfully to him.

"I can't have you use those references," I told him. To assuage my anger with him, I took his white hand and caressed it against my cheek.

"You are overwrought, my poor dear," he smiled. "God, how I love temperament after the milk and water creatures I live with. But understand, the Bird of Heaven is my great-grandson. He is also the supreme emotional attachment of my career. He was given the name Bird—"

Here I began writhing as if with intolerable pain, but Elijah continued:

"—the name was given him by his colored servant and nurse. Because of my love for him, I am all but barred from ever seeing the boy. He is supervised by a guardian as hellish and low-down as Millicent De Frayne herself. Damn these duennas of the world who keep decent parties apart!" he cried, and he began walking about the room, beating his breast, arranging a loose earring, and making breathing sounds like a badly spent swimmer.

Turning on me suddenly, he cried, "I won't be bossed by you, smitten as I am by your absolutely overpowering personality . . . And furthermore, mark this down, you have got to give that harpy of a woman up, do you hear . . . And I want an explanation of this feather," he cried, in a towering rage. But he had forgotten his rage was only white. Taking his proffered white hand, I bit it again and again, while his piercing screams echoed through the building. He fell against me, then, and we lay there, becoming calm, comforting one another.

Hours later, as he bade me a warm embrace of a good-bye, I made him promise me that he would not force me to give up Millicent De Frayne.

"You will never know, Albert, how many concessions you have wrung from me in one day of our wonderful friendship. I have committed treason against myself all for your sake. You are in the pay, as spy, of my mortal enemy, and yet I go along with that. You forbid me to give the only name I have ever used for my great-grandson, and I seem to go along there too."

"I will stop my ears, and let you say his name," I pampered him. But even as he said *Bird of Heaven*, while I stopped my ears, I shivered and shook, and the beads of sweat gathered again on my whole body of "ripe eggplant."

Perhaps because I was growing old, though the vigor of my veins and skin made me look youthful, I seemed to require the company of ancient Elijah and Millicent. They made me feel dawn-young. There had to be, however, and this was wrung from them with the greatest difficulty, several periods of several hours each week in which I boarded the Staten Island ferryboat and went to the zoo, where I patiently transacted some business in one of the buildings.

I do not know who resented most these absences, Millicent or Elijah. Had I gone to the Cameroons, they could not have been more edgy. "You have no right to go so far!" both used the same expression, as I was later to find out they often employed the identical favorite phrases, words, idioms. After all they had been enemies for longer than most people occupy the same body, in this life.

If you think he's wonderful now, wait till the snow flies!" Millicent said after she had listened to my account of my visit. "When the Arcturus Gardens opens for the winter recital season, you'll see," she began, but suddenly she was laughing, and for a moment I mistook these sounds actually for some mechanical disturbance in the apartment, for her laugh was entirely unhuman sounding. "Until you have seen him dance, you know nothing of him. He's only himself when he lets the crocus curtain rise, and he's Adonis or Pierrot, or Narcissus . . . Of course I pay for it all, you understand."

"He denies you give him a penny."

She smoothed the folds of a leather pouch, and then carefully opened it. Inside was a gold beaded purse with a dazzling fastener. When she opened it, one heard a sound like a pistol going off. She extricated from it a huge feather.

"You must have dropped this from your own person as you left the other day," she spoke in a voice distant like an echo over water. "Pray, come and take it, for I doubt not you'll need it, my pet."

It seemed that I was unable to rise from the chair in order to come and take the proffered feather, so long did I remain immobile. At last with the greatest difficulty, she rose and approached me. She put the feather behind my ear, for it was an immense one, and then, much in the manner of Elijah Thrush, she took a large shimmering handkerchief and wiped my upper lip of moisture.

All that summer, from deserted warehouses, and other empty buildings near ghastly grisly West Street, with its rotting refuse and dying derelicts wearing burlap shoes, with the green façade of old pier entrances in the distance, I followed Elijah Thrush in his nocturnal and diurnal wanderings. For here he did emerge at times, whether to find a new disciple, at which he was often successful, or merely to sell some of his old watercolors, or just to review his impressions of the outside world. But West Street, with its drifters and addicts, its soul-food restaurants, its memories of great boats leaving for Europe, was as illogical and impossible of belief as the Arcturus Gardens. And when Elijah at last appeared here in his long saffron robes, his shoulder-length hair, and rattling jewelry, he evoked very few surprised looks from the other denizens. Nonetheless he knew *I* was spying on him, and I had to undergo later hours of recrimination from him, bitter scoldings, venomous taunts and insults. After which I would have to pose stark naked for him, a practice I first vigorously opposed, owing to certain connections my bare body had with my habit, despite my protective jeweled stomacher, but he would not allow refusal. However, he did go over my body as if with a magnifying glass, and kept giving vent to his surprise, not only at my fantastic "development," but at strange yellow discolorations, which I blamed the sun for.

One torpid afternoon, when the atmosphere weighed so heavy one felt floating in a sack of stale water, I followed the Mime at a rather unsafe closeness (I did not know then or now if he saw me pursuing him) to a huge granite building with a sign of crumbling gold:

THE ALIMENTARY FOUNDATION
A HOME FOR THE UNWANTED

Here before a barred window the Mime came to an abrupt halt, then looking all about him carefully, like a pickpocket who must see if anybody is watching, he opened his handbag and drew out a looking glass, some boxes of cosmetic, and a large broken horn comb. He touched up his eyebrows, eyelashes, and sideburns with mascara, painted his mouth, especially on the lower lip, and put two rouge spots on his cheeks, then gave a cursory going over of his black hair with the comb. He then relaxed his facial muscles so that he would appear at his best, and, having put away his reticule, clapped his hands peremptorily.

An elderly woman in a cerise wig, with bowed back, came out from a side door which I had failed to observe before, and Elijah handed her over some dollar bills, but did not so much as look at her, let alone exchange two words. Hardly had the crone gotten back into the building than there came a grinding sound as the barred window before which he stood opened, and there appeared a young boy with flowing raven locks, haunting wild Indian eyes, and a mouth of brilliant vermilion: a striking family resemblance in the boy's every feature to Elijah Thrush.

Then there began an apostrophe such as I have never heard from human lips. (Indeed, I was so overwrought by this outpouring of "hopeless love" that I had to lean against the building for support.)

"Dear Bird of Heaven," he began, "realer to me than life or dream," and for a brief moment I thought he was singing, "kept as in a cage, away from me who love you. I who out of the entire world alone care for your tiniest discomfort. Yes, my precious," and he stopped speaking, for some makeup had seemingly got in his left eye and he had to wait to remove it before continuing. "Here we are, kept asunder like two dangerous criminals . . . Do you hear me, Bird? Have they been speaking against me again in there, condemning and sullying my name to you? As if the Shepherd of the Flock would betray the Lamb of the Flock!"

The young boy now leaned out as far as he could through the bars, and made kissing sounds, sounds which at the same time resembled oh so closely the calls of mating birds.

"If you only knew what it means to me to hear your song of response, after days of not seeing you, Bird!" Elijah drew as close to the bars as he could, and at that moment the boy allowed his hand to reach to the Mime's outstretched arm.

"Do you love me, my dearest being?" Elijah cried, but even as he said this, he dropped the hand of the boy, agitated beyond belief, for he was aware of a change of light in the Bird's room, and a heavy shadow moved close now to the window.

"Tell me while we still have some little seconds left, my child, if you reciprocate my love."

The Bird now made two kissing sounds in rapid succession (which I was later to learn meant *yes*), but at the same moment, the great shadow which had been approaching the boy grew large enough to engulf the entire window, and there was a sudden loud resounding bang as the wooden shutter closed on the street separating the lovers.

Elijah fell on his knees before the barred window, resembling, it seemed to me, a Spanish lover of ages past, serenading his mistress, and only lacking the guitar.

I was so engrossed by this scene of hopeless love that, forgetting I was a paid spy, I went up to Elijah and helped raise him up from the pavement.

He too had forgotten that I was not supposed to be here, that my presence betokened betrayal, for he greeted me effusively, and held me close to him, while his tears joined themselves to my drops of sweat, in little rivulets, down my cheeks.

"You have discovered me in the one great love of my life, Albert," he said, as we began to walk away from the "prison," "and the irony of it all, which is the irony of my life of course, is that instead of being able to act out my love, I must stand here before a barred window like an outlaw and grovel in the dirt. I know they are mistreating the child, for he's growing paler by the day.

"He is a mute, Albert," he went on, and then stopped walking to look me directly in the eye. "My beloved great-grandson cannot speak one syllable. Yet he knows and understands all I say to him. He is a brilliant child, and realizes I love him with all my heart."

Turning back to the window now, he brandished a clenched muscular fist against the sign reading

THE ALIMENTARY FOUNDATION

"They vetoed me long ago. I speak of the authorities of course, Albert," the Mime tried to speak calmly. "I was forbidden to raise the boy on the grounds that as a great artist I am bound to be a leper, not fit for the company of my own flesh and blood. This is the kind of land we inhabit, you and I, Albert, the philistine empire of critics, money-men and haters of the human heart.

But even as Elijah, prior to bidding me goodbye, had been telling me I now shared the great secret of his life, the Bird, I had begun to go off woolgathering, and was in a deep study about my own mastering private trouble, and when I had snapped to, he had already departed and gone back to his studio, and the "cold government of reason." His banishment on moral grounds from association with his great-grandson made me begin to half-agree with the Mime, that we two were connected in a "mystical real way," and the bare outlines of our life were not too dissimilar.

I was brought back suddenly to a humiliation of my own with a white man who contrasted sharply with Elijah Thrush, for whatever failings the Mime may have had, and however great his deep-down prejudice, he had taken me as I was, and held me responsible for loving him with all his heart, and no excuse of skin color or previous history or condition were countenanced. On the other hand my relationship with Ted Maufritz, a retired liberal-radical, is not so excusable to me to this day. This white gentleman of a wealthy banking family had the custom of making me lie down on a velvet couch, protected from stains by goat skin and plastic throws. He would then open one of my best veins and drink a considerable amount of my blood in the hope, he said, and only in the hope of being "worthy" of the noble race I was scion of. "Remember me when yours will be the power and glory of this world," he would cry intoxicated by my physical prowess.

Although my loss of blood may not have been deleterious to my constitution, I would have continued, I believe, with "unworthy" Ted Maufritz, allowing him to approach the rising star of my own race, had not one evening when I had stripped routinely to allow him to open one of my veins, by chance another of the large feathers was discovered stuck to my badly sweating breast.

Ted Maufritz flew into such a terrible seizure of rage he was unable to partake of even a half ounce of my blood, though there I lay bleeding for him, since he had already opened the vein.

We parted friends on his part, however, though he had been injudicious enough to call me a *jamoka* during his greatest anger. I allowed him however to shake hands with me after I was clothed.

I had had "chambers" near Trinity Church, in the Wall Street area of Manhattan Island, but shortly after I was cashiered by Ted Maufritz, and without a red cent in my pocket, I had another fearful surprise when Juddson, the overseer of my private rooms, told me of a new ruling which had come about that those now occupying the special habitations could no longer use them for the purpose of sleeping or preparing food. Needless to say the "chambers" were the place I had recourse to for my habit, but I had always spent the night there also on the floor. And so from now on when night came I would find myself like any vagrant, without a place to lay my weary head.

I tongue-lashed white Juddson, and went out. A few short years ago, he would have stung me with a pejorative, but now owing to my brothers' victories he could only bite his pale lips and let me go.

This was when I made up my mind I would have to be Millicent's spy. During my first weeks of shadowing Elijah I had nowhere to sleep, and did not wish to impart knowledge of my lack of shelter to either her or the Mime.

My trouble at this time was not, however, so much a lack of place to sleep, as a new malady which has no more a name than does my habit. I was falling not merely under the spell of Elijah Thrush, I was deeply in love with him.

"Of course I foresaw it," Millicent explained to me, one early August morning. (She got up about five o'clock in the morning and surveyed the heavens carefully; it was her only real pleasure.) "It either results that the spy falls in love with Elijah or he quits his post . . ."

Suddenly enriched by my fortuitous contact with Millicent De Frayne, I bought a silk suit and registered at the Divine Fairgroves Hotel, where my "princely" appearance secured for me one of the finer sleeping rooms with a view of the river, and a seat in the dining room very near the table at which Father Divine had eaten in this life and where his ghostly presence visits regularly even now. It was also easier for Millicent De Frayne to leave messages for me at so respectable a lodging place.

I do not know whether to say that from this time onwards my progress was upward or downward. Had I not become an impressed spy for Millicent De Frayne, and the lover of the spiritual world of Elijah Thrush, I might, it seems to me in quiet hours, have given up the expense of my habit, and become any black man trying to find his bread, but then there is, as Elijah said, destiny. My destiny was, certainly, first to be afflicted with the grandiloquence of my habit, for it is the only one, I believe, of its kind, and secondly and in a circle with it, the intoxicating presence of these larger-than-life people, Millicent and Elijah.

I soon discovered that Millicent was deceiving me. One August noon she told me that I could have a few days rest, and during this time I would not need to pay calls on the Mime. This was a command, I saw at once. Her hand trembled as she passed me the dish of tea. She covered the veins of her neck higher and higher with her furs. She never looked me in the eye.

"You are the kindest of ladies," I told her.

"You don't mean a word of that."

"Millicent, Millicent," I took the boldest course now by calling her by her Christian white name.

She placed her right hand heavy with several rings over the bridge of her immense aquiline nose, and as this nose was now covered, for the first time I realized what it

resembled. I became almost immediately ill, putting the
delicate tea cup down with a rough bang.

"You must forgive me," she took away her hand, but
I could not for a moment bear to look at her.

"Do you know hopeless love, Albert Peggs?"

"Yes, all forms," I sobbed. "All forms of hopeless."

"How remarkable, yes how perfectly remarkable," she
soothed me. "Sit over here, my dear, on the little tabouret."

I sipped a bit more of the tea, and then did as she bid me.

"You must go away for a few days. You need rest."
I shook now convulsively. I heard a kind of pulling
movement, then felt my own hand raised, and something
rudely pushed on the second finger of the left hand. I
opened my eyes and saw she had put one of her own
pearl rings upon this finger.

"Don't say what you have ready to say. If the doorman
notices the ring on the finger, and stops you, have him
call me of course. It is yours, Albert, provided you are
absent for a few days . . . What was the nature of your
hopeless love?" she inquired.

"I admired a certain party," I said.

"What color was he?"

"White," I told her.

"How destiny grinds us to powder," she said. "Can you
wipe your face, Albert?"

From my table in the dining room of the Divine Fairgroves Hotel, I spent most of the day afterwards admiring the ring she had given me. I had never felt stronger, and
I had never felt more ill. I think I thought I was dying,
while gaining strength. I felt at times I had died and gone
to white heaven, and that Elijah and Millicent were God

and Goddess there, keepers of a park, and I was their Only Son. Yet my real destiny, I knew, lay in my rented "chambers."

I stationed myself outside on the fire escape of Elijah Thrush's Arcturus Gardens. I felt Millicent would come by daylight, for after six in the evening when she had her poached mackerel and capers, she was too sleepy to go out, and she was only actually conscious for a few daylight hours.

She came at high noon, while the sun broiled down on me. I suppose they knew I was outside, and for that very reason both she and he walked to within earshot of where I stood. My discomfort was more than rewarded.

"Many as the time I've had that lock changed to keep you out, you always are able to get a key that fits, and come in like the robber of my time and perfection which you are," Elijah's voice came to me. He was seated at the piano, playing a few notes, and I knew the person he addressed was Millicent, "You look even older than when you barged in here a month ago!"

"You never change," Millicent's voice rose, as if from cobwebs. "More adorable than ever, Elijah."

"Stop those ridiculous caresses."

"When shall we be married?"

"When hell freezes its oldest star boarders."

I heard someone cover someone with scores of kisses, and a feeble cry of dissatisfaction and loathing came from the Mime . . .

"It's bad enough when you put your claws in those of

us who have weapons to fight you back with," Elijah
spoke again, "but when you choose as your victim a
poor lad of another race who cannot fight back . . ."

"Poor lad, my eye . . . He's a mature man of twenty-
nine, and strong as a brace of dray horses."

"Ah, but he looks like an infant. I don't believe he has
a beard as yet!"

"Well, he has enough feathers about his person, if you
ask me, to more than make up for a pair of smooth
cheeks!"

"Oh, I'd nearly forgotten those damnable feathers,"
Elijah cried with a start. "What do you suppose they
mean?" he assumed a casual tone now, as if forgetting
he was speaking with his eternal enemy.

"After all, he must have cannibal blood, don't you
suppose?" Millicent dismissed the subject. Then after a
pause: "Do you know everything I say offends him. I
adore him, but I can't bring my caring across to him.
He has a skin of the finest mahogany, and his eyes break
my heart—almond-shaped, you know. Many an hour after
he has left I weep because his physical perfection is still
so persistent in the room, the draperies, and furniture
where he has been . . ."

"You doddering ninny!" Elijah roared. "How can you
expect Albert to give so much as one of his toenails for an
advanced old thing like you!"

Millicent laughed. "If age were a barrier from his point
of view, my darling, he wouldn't be as soft on you as
he is. You didn't know? Well, he's smitten with you to
the point of mistaking you for a white god and all that.
All one has to do is mention your name and he's all
calf eyes . . . But through money, he'll betray you. He'll
turn you in just when you've gone all overboard for him."

"You've delivered your last speech in this studio, old

muff!" Elijah cried, hoarse with anger. "Belamy," he called to the piano player, "come in here and put this chattering jay into the street!"

Their quarreling over me intoxicated me. Their praise of my body, my soul, my qualities known and unknown made me unable to restrain myself. Removing all I had on I entered by the fire-escape window, and came in to offer my love to them, holding my clothes in my left hand.

They paid not the slightest attention to me. Their quarrel, which had after all been going on since 1913, could not be interrupted by a naked nigger, I slowly began to see.

"Put on a dressing gown, Albert, you'll come down with a bug sure as fate," Millicent found time to speak to me, while Belamy helped her on with her hat, and with her permission wiped a crooked streak of rouge off her mouth, caused, I learned later, by the Mime's striking her across the mouth.

"Don't be nicer to him than you have to, my child!" Millicent warned me, as the door closed on her.

I turned at once to Elijah, hoping for more praise, more words of love from him.

He did not even look at me. Seated at the piano, he was playing a selection from Gottschalk, and each succeeding time I attempted to gain his attention he turned away from me.

I was not doing it for the money because I do not know how to do anything for money, but the money came, kept coming, was more than plentiful. "We'll do it in this little surreptitious way," Millicent always phrased it, as she pressed crisp hundred-dollar bills into my palm, and always marveled it was wet with exertion. "You're worried about something, my dear," she would say. "Is it Alabama?"

Elijah also chided me. "You do not keep your mind completely on what I am saying to you, or on the major importance of my personality, Albert . . . You are making your fortune through me, 'tis true, and you know as well as you're sitting in that Beauvais chair, you belong to me, heart and soul . . . Yet nevertheless there's somebody else! I've known it from the beginning . . . There, there you're driveling again in that abominable way. You can look really ugly when you do that . . . Oh, Albert, why can't you give me total fidelity, total oneness." He shaded his face with his long rather red fingers, with the slightly unclean nails.

*E*lijah has told me there is somebody else," Millicent also now broached this subject. She seemed more perturbed than he was. She was wearing pink shoes with enormous gold buckles on them, and owing to an attack of rheumatism she held her head far forward so that she gave the impression she was talking into a low-lying dumb-waiter. "He was most abusive to me on the telephone today, but then his fury turned on you, Albert . . . He knows there's somebody else in your life . . ."

"Not exactly a someone," I finally broke my own promise to myself to be mum and let this out.

Despite the pain of her aching bones and neck, she got her head up and stared at me. "There shouldn't, there mustn't be!" she protested.

"But I have had my . . . attachment before I met you!"
I cried, a little.

"But my dear, I thought we—that is, Elijah and I—
were your all, were certainly supposed to be your all."

"There is . . . somebody else," I finally put it their
way, for I could not make a clean breast of my dilemma,
my attachment, whatever you might call it. I thought of
where I had been born in Alabama, Bon Secour, and the
towns of my grandfather and great-grandfather, Atmore,
Canoe, and Tunnel Springs.

"Attention here, attention!" I heard Millicent's voice.
"Oh, how you woolgather these last few weeks, Albert.
It's broken my heart. If you go back on me, I don't
know of any way of reaching him (Elijah), and it may
be the end of the line. You have an overexaggeration of
what money can do. It does nothing. No woman ever
lived from the Garden of Eden down who has suffered
as I suffer. I live on and on, and each day is more
penible. He said a very cutting thing to me today, I
think the most discouraging and cutting thing ever said
to me. I felt I had been relegated, somehow, to a dusty
attic . . . Draw close, my dear, for I don't want one of
the servants to overhear . . ."

As I approached her chair, she whispered . . . "Do you
know what I sit on, Albert, my child, according to the
Mime?" Tears ran down her cheeks bearing with them
the same brand of French rouge the Mime wore; indeed
I was to learn later she bought him all his cosmetics.

"Come, come, Albert, you've been to the university,
only a year, 'tis true, but that's more than most folks get,
no matter what their lineage."

"It will take some time to guess, Millicent," I warned
her.

"Don't we have forever? . . . At least I do."

She drew me to her, and a drop of cosmetic fell on my wrist. She immediately dried it with a man-sized handkerchief. "Listen closely. He said I sit on a *tuffet* here—" She pointed with one sweep of her hand to indicate that her chair was placed on a raised platform. "Do you hear the fiendish spite in the choice of that word? Tuffet!"

I grinned gapingly and she looked at me with searching pupils.

"I have no idea what will have to be done with your other attachment. He told me he will not go on with you unless you give up this other person . . ."

"But there is no other person . . ."

"Albert, you are far too handsome not to have paramours," she contradicted me.

"Oh, well, those." I sat down on a tiny stool on her "tuffet," and then at the thought of the word she had employed—"paramours"—I could not help laughing outright.

"Go ahead, be coarse and low," she said. "But you'll find no pity or understanding from Elijah. And he'll make my life a hell until you make a clean breast of all this. Where, for example, do you go when you are not with your own people at the Divine Fairgroves Hotel, Albert . . ."

"Is nothing to be left private in my life . . ."

"We have investigated nothing about you, you know that, Albert," she was quite hurt now, and rang for the maid.

"I took you on first seeing you because of an intuition, and because of your marvelous eyes. Also your breath is sweet as orange-blossom honey, to tell you the truth, that's what made me decide on you . . . Norah," she addressed the entering servant, "bring a tray with one of the better cordials, and, wait a moment, don't rush out like a chicken with severed jugular, for pity's sake, kindly fetch two of the cut-glass wine goblets, the larger ones, if you please, and wait a minute, stop right there, don't rush so, I want a water biscuit with my cordial. Now, you can rush, and I hope you will . . . That woman loathes me, Albert," she commented when the servant left. "I've found literature in her sleeping room, she's a popular religionist of some kind and believes the world is drawing to an early close. Hence her lofty phlegm with me."

"I suppose you and Elijah would be surprised if I spilled my own semen on the floor before you, for your entertainment, of course, and you would be surprised it was not brown!" I stood up as I delivered this statement.

"How perfectly droll," she considered my words, which I had uttered hardly knowing I was even going to speak, and was as surprised, no, more surprised than she when I heard what I said. "You seem not to have learned the first lesson of our first encounter. I have no interest in any race, least of all the human race. I would be quite content living with baboons, except they are said to have an objectionable disposition, but probably no worse than that religious tomfool of a Norah, who loves Jesus, and yet can't abide her own mistress who gives her her bread."

"What if I told you I was in love with a bird?" I let the words out, as I pulled at her gown.

"Albert," she went on, as if I had not spoken, "one afternoon a few weeks ago, a piece of paper, with your own handwriting, fell out of your pants pocket. I picked it up with some difficulty, but I did not want the maid to find anything which might turn her more against me, and also against you, and I will return it to you, if you wish it. I have it in safe custody upstairs. The paper said, 'Are white griefs true, are they real.' I could not get this sentence out of my mind for a long time. But I have the answer for you, Albert. They are. They're real. You won't believe it, but God knows it to be a fact . . . Now a moment ago you spoke in very concrete sexual terms. You must get out of your noble head that either Elijah or I want your body, exquisite and noble as its lines are, and I have many an afternoon marveled at the curves of your arms and thighs. I have made every mistake known to the human mind, so can scarcely have a shred of prudery. We do not want your semen, to use your curious way of describing your gift to the white world. We want your soul."

Just as Millicent did not hear certain of my statements, I do not think I quite caught this statement. However, later in the Divine Fairgroves Hotel (where tears filled my eyes so frequently, that I had finally to make the excuse to my brothers I had hay fever, though actually fall was passing into winter) I went over all Millicent had told me about myself, and herself, and Elijah . . .

"You will not have met the Mime until the snow flies, remember! For it's then he opens the Arcturus Gardens, and dances publicly!" her words came back to me, as inadvertently I opened my purse and allowed four thousand-dollar bills to fall before the eyes of the astonished waitress. "I have come into an inheritance," I explained as I looked up into her inquisitive face.

At that very moment Millicent De Frayne was talking to Elijah Thrush on the telephone. "He tells me he is in love with a bird."

"My dear, either your mind has gone this time, and they will be calling for you shortly, which will be a blessed relief to human kind everywhere, or they have punctured your eardrum as revenge, those hellish servants of yours . . . When your brain has cleared, communicate with my piano player if you have anything of import to convey. And send me some money, do you hear, miserly creature that you are!"

"He thinks all we want is his semen," Millicent continued the conversation, but there was a click-click of the wire as the Mime hung up on her.

"I should have died in 1917," Millicent sat with the pink and gold cradle of the phone resting in her lap. "I wish it were the month of tulips. I loathe fall flowers, with their indeterminate foliage, and their lobed leaves. I would give anything for a roomful of tulips. I think it would make me happy."

Millicent De Frayne had not actually grown any older since 1913, because in that year having fallen in love with Elijah Thrush, who was billed at the Hippodrome theater as "The Most Beautiful Man in the World," each day succeeding their first back-stage meeting, she had done nothing but think of the impossibility of their love. He had half-encouraged her to take up a lifetime devoted to unrequited passion, and this half-encouragement was more than any other human being had ever given her.

As the frost of winter hung in the air, Millicent acknowledged the coming cold weather by one change in her dress, she put on her pearl choker. She did not put on any more furs than she wore in July.

Both Millicent and the Mime were in a state of preternatural excitement now that he was appearing again before the footlights, albeit both the presentation of his work, and his audience (since it was a merely invited, not a paying one), had very little if anything to do with the New York theater season.

"New York, dearest Albert," Millicent spoke to me from her crimson seat on the tuffet, "is over. Has been over actually since 1917, but we have indulged it to the extent of pretending it was continuing. I suppose you will be going back to that town in Alabama, what did you say the name of it was . . . Atmore, Canoe, or Coffee Springs, or Burnt Corn, or one of those names. I have been looking at the map of your state, and if the places are as interesting as the names, I might winter there. But when New York ends, you will, I assume, go back to Alabama.

"Albert!" she cried now in great splenetic irritability. "Your eyes are glazed with inattention."

"I beg your pardon, Millicent," I told her. "I am very depressed today."

"If I could only understand your depression . . ."

Norah came forward now with a tiny golden tray, two alfalfa tablets, and a beaker of water. Millicent frowned as she took the tablets and drank as thirstily from the beaker as if she were a horse.

"He claims," Millicent suddenly began paraphrasing from a recently opened letter, "that if he is not beautiful this season, and the audience does not love him to perfection, he will kill himself . . . As you know, I am forbidden to attend any of his performances . . ."

I was a farmer's son, believe it or scoff at my confession, if you will," Elijah Thrush told me, to prepare me, in a sense, for his Grand Opening at the Arcturus Gardens. "My father had been a farmer in Illinois, and then the family decided for some reason unknown to me to go to the plains of Montana. Here I would have remained forever, my dear Albert, following a horse's

backside around a field of buckwheat, had I not gone
to the Grand Opera House one evening, and seen a
troupe of dancers who had come along with the produc-
tion of *Carmen*. I knew then I would leave my religious
parents and go to Chicago. I was fifteen. Though I loved
my dad dearly, for he had always put up with my pranks,
my mother, who was a religious maniac, opposed anything that was not hard labor and prayer. Without a
goodbye to them, I hopped a freight, on which I got a
job watching the livestock, and arrived in Chicago with
four dollars in my pants pocket, and without knowing a
soul in town . . . But my personality was already fully
developed, and if you will allow me to say so, though I
know I am a bit dilapidated by current standards, I won
the hearts of all who met me. Indeed, I had hardly gone
two blocks down Michigan Avenue when a noted impre-
sario of that age called Adams saw me and immediately
booked me as a youth who carries banners in some
Shakespeare plays—they were *Henry VI*, parts I and II
and III. But I soon tired of parts, and shipping steerage to
Greece, I made my debut on the steps of the Parthenon
. . . Then Paris . . ."

I was retelling this story every now and again to
Millicent De Frayne, although she had heard it all a
thousand times from the lips of the Mime, and from her
own copious notebooks . . .

"That was the way it was," she responded and raised
her head from sleep, and nodded, smiling.

"Look outside," she cried, a kind of awe coming over
her. "It's snowing. Summer is over, and the season has
begun! Do you hear me, Albert . . . The Arcturus
Gardens will be opening any minute now . . ."

Yes, it was snowing, huge great flakes of the stuff, so
foreign to my skin and heart, and yet in my veins summer

raged more fierce than ever, and my upper lip was ever covered with a kind of pool of sweat which no matter how many times Millicent commanded me or a servant to wipe dry, oozed out again like a great punctured artery. She despaired of me. But her mind was on his opening, and so she neglected me. She had her finest gowns brought out and ordered new pumps. The jeweler was sent for, and new chokers looked at, and a new ring purchased.

"Understand, I will not be admitted," she told me. "Not because I will arrive two hours late, but for the principle of the thing. He must reject me, he must drive me out especially in front of his public. I have ruined his life, and this must be told to the public. And I will be as humiliated and abashed as if it were all real. Yes, Albert, white griefs are real, though you deny us substance."

"I never said . . ."

"You wrote it though, and I will hold that letter of yours in a place of safety until this whole city is ashes." A terrible passion seemed to shake her.

"You are taken care of," she cried, almost breathless. "But who ever took care of me. *You* know slavery? Fool! What of the slavery I have known. Now sit," she told me as I approached her tuffet. "You must not miss one detail of his performance tonight." And there was her calendar lying open, commanding: Sunday, November 28.

Although Millicent had fortified me before my first visit to the Arcturus Gardens with cold guinea sandwiches, Liebfraumilch, strong coffee and brandy, my knees were water as I knocked at the door of Elijah's private theater, waiting to be ushered into my new life—for my knowing Elijah only socially as a spy of Millicent De Frayne was no preparation at all for seeing him in his reincarnation as the Most Beautiful Man in the World. Knocking then, and waiting, I felt most unlike myself, though I had been getting less like myself ever since that July interview with Millicent. I was wrapped in one of her fourth husband's heavy fur coats. A reverend crone opened the tall door, and inquired my name. A second crone, white-haired, profusely powdered, with tiny jet earrings, looked over the first old lady's shoulder.

She went down the list of those invited to the performance but could not find the name of Albert Peggs.

"But I have been sent by Millicent De Frayne!" I cried, so that some of the early audience inside the small theater began clearing their throats.

"I can assure you," Mother Macaulay, the first white-haired lady, spoke in feeling tones of indignation, "I can doubly assure you that no friend of Millicent De Frayne can be admitted here."

"After all the money she has sent the Mime," I wondered aloud.

"She has never so much as given him a red penny," the second lady spoke up. "Will you be so kind as to depart, young sir."

"There is nobody in the world," I raised my lungs so that I would be heard throughout the building, "nobody anywhere who loves and respects Elijah Thrush as much as I. I will not take no for an answer, and I will not depart." I pushed my way past them just in time to hear the old familiar stentor cry, "Allow him the big plush throne seat, Mother Macaulay, in the first row, and for God's sake will you and Abigail Tuttle cease your bickering. Can glory never come without being clouded by incompetent devotees? Go to your places as soon as he's seated, and tonight admit everybody. Turn away nobody, do you hear?"

"And should Miss De Frayne show up tonight?" Mother

Macaulay inquired, smarting under the corrosive things he had said about her tonight.

"Admit that molting old harum-scarum too, if she can haul her bones through this snowstorm," Elijah's voice began to fade, but not before I had cried out toward where the voice was proceeding, "Thank you, dearest friend, for providing for me." I thought I heard a kiss blown toward me in reply.

Yes, outside it was snowing thickly, but in here, it was too warm, and there was a most powerful perfume, scent of vetiver, and thick clouds of Kashmir Saffron and Quaipur Rose incense which almost at once made my eyelids hazy.

A kind of burning like naphtha had been eating within my veins, but suddenly here I began to shiver, so that I did not remove my heavy coat though Mother Macaulay several times advanced toward me and made motions indicating she would take the burden of it from me, should I desire it.

The small theater was now filled, and I had time to look at the walls covered with gold-framed paintings of the Mime's middle-period in oils. The paintings depicted the Mime as Hiawatha, the child Moses, Apollo, and Jesus in the Garden with Mary Magdalene, in addition to a long gallery of portraits of seraphic young men. As I was gazing at these, an old woman next to me leaned over and spoke. "Those are his dead amours," she whispered. "They all went the same way," and she shook her head several times and frowned. "They failed him," she was about to go on, when a gong sounded, and the lights began to grow weak.

In the distance I heard a deep sorrowful voice praying.

Then a hand was clapped and in a lightning second (indeed, I thought a ball of fireworks had been thrown on the

stage) the Mime, Elijah himself, was before my startled
eyeballs, looking not more than twenty-five years old,
and I suppose, despite his atrocious jewelry and makeup,
as handsome as the gods on the wall. He made kissing
sounds to all.

Whether it was because my illness grew exacerbated by
the incense, or owing to sheer excitement, I felt it wise
to slump to the floor so as not to excite my nerves more
than I knew they would be excited by what I was to
undergo, and I allowed my head to rest against the boots
of a young white gentleman who told me not to think
of formality but to make myself comfortable, and as if
prompted already by either Elijah or Millicent De Frayne
he began wiping my upper lip over which swam ice-cold
drops.

After Elijah's first electric appearance, which thrilled
everybody into a cascade of vehement applause, Mother
Macaulay mounted the stage and announced the Mime's
first number, after having given the short biographical
sketch of which I have already apprised any reader of
this narrative, the number in question being *Narcissus
Drinks His Last Glass of Joy*.

In this selection Elijah was clothed only in a cherry-
colored throw.

"Just think, he is over ninety," the youth against whose
boots I was reclining said. I was too ill to reply in words,
but since my hands were always strong, I tugged at his
laces instead.

I now almost began to wonder if this was actually Elijah,
for if he was ninety or seventy or a hundred, his body was
as firm as an apple, and his genitals looked as hopeful as
those of someone expecting to raise a large number of
children. Still, it was his profession never to look the
same from one moment to the next.

An entr'acte now followed, in which the young man who sat behind me, having taken a fondness for me, I suppose, because of my African personality, plied me with some cognac from his private phial. "I always find someone here rewarding," he said. "I never miss a season." "What do you do for a liv—" I was about to ask when the gong sounded again and the lights went out.

I have nearly in my relived excitement of that night forgotten to tell the reader that Eugene Belamy, the pianist, was in full evening dress, looking terribly New York, with handsome dark circles in his moon-pale face, and a geranium in his buttonhole, and flashing looks of malevolent hatred at me when he was not playing Cécile Chaminade or Eric Coates.

"Are you a bosom friend of the Mime?" the young man whispered in my ear. "I feel I am losing consciousness," I told him, "you may have to care for me." But my lightheadedness didn't seem to alarm me somehow or my companion either, who merely went on humming the tunes he heard played on the piano.

Several numbers now must have taken place, *Pierrot*, I recall, an interminable one in a French garden, in which the Mime wore green tights, and finally a sensual débâcle called *Bacchanal in the Sahara Desert*, where the Mime wore dromedary bells which only, alas, reminded me so much of the Salvation Army at Christmas time that its undoubted beauty was lost on me.

But in the midst of this number, a terrible crash was heard at the door and, true to promise, Millicent De Frayne entered, with a young man dressed as a fireman, carrying an axe. He had broken down the door of course— all the regular audience realized at once he was not a bona fide member of the fire department.

"Stop this uncalled-for performance at once!" Millicent's cry reached me. I was stupefied, for was this the way to treat a man you had loved since 1913. "Stop it, I say!" she roared. And she looked so remarkably young, too, there was not a trace of her rheumatism or indeed her eighty-odd years. My illness seemed to abate, and I sat up, still on the floor, hoping, idly, I suppose, to be recognized by her, for she was so magnificent and arresting I hoped she would salute me before all these interesting people.

"Damned old bag of bones, stomping in like this in the midst of my most fatiguing number . . . Ladies and gentlemen, this common whore here, kept out of jail only by her wealth, which she never earned a dime of, has been persecuting me since the turn of the century. (In his anger he always gave away his age, though professionally he listed himself always as twenty-eight.) She has the breath of a tribe of cannibals and about as much beauty as an overage anteater, yet she flatters herself that I am hopelessly enamored of her . . . She even gives out that she is supporting me in this theater! Can you believe it, friends and public!" (There were very enthusiastic cries of *No*, as in a rehearsed play.)

"On the other hand, this wicked mountebank," Millicent De Frayne began her rejoinder, "has corrupted his own great-grandson, and there is not a young person in this audience tonight whom he has not either corrupted or will ruin and corrupt. I am begging you therefore to run as you would for your lives, run indeed as if the whole edifice were in flames . . . Ancient Antinoüs! I hate what you've done to us all," she now addressed the Mime directly, and she brought out a large fantastically long knife, and rushed at him.

He seized Millicent at once, removing the knife from her

yellow hands, and then spat without real feeling or force in her face.

While this was going on, I had not realized that the young man next to me had almost entirely undressed me. My overcoat was gone, and my trousers and shorts had disappeared. Thinking he was about to enjoy my body, I turned to question him but he had of course disappeared.

The evening now began to have a lengthy quality like church service, certainly more undivided attention was required than for regular entertainment, for instead of the scheduled performance of Mime, we were given in its place a series of solo dances by Millicent De Frayne, who wore under her opera cloak a complete suit of armor, so that she looked like Boadicea, according to several spectators.

She did at least four, perhaps half a dozen numbers, distressing to watch, since she had trouble raising her feet, and besides all during her entertainment the Mime was booing and catcalling from the wings, and shouting things like "A scarecrow in a high wind would have more grace!" and "You can't hear the piano for her bones creaking!"

At the end of her various numbers, Millicent, who was beginning to win a good deal of applause, as an encore had just begun to sing the ballad

> "Oh, if the moon had been shining,
>   And the lilacs in bloom,
>   But 'twas pouring with rain, my lovely,
>   'Twas pouring—"

when the Mime, unable any longer to be standing unheralded in the wings, leaped out and seized Millicent for his partner, and began doing an unparalleled two-step with her, to the fresh enthusiasm of the audience, for it was suddenly apparent she needed only his guiding hand to be brilliant. Indeed, their duo bid fair to be the hit of the season at the Arcturus Gardens when suddenly, from the back of the theater, somebody shouted, "Po-lice!" Purple in the face and puffing from their exertions, Millicent and Elijah nonetheless danced on, gliding into a tango. The bluecoats had arrived through the broken front door, with their nightsticks twirling, and, thinking they could only be coming for me, I dashed bare-assed for the fire esape, and then just as I was descending I heard gunfire . . .

I remained away from Millicent De Frayne and Elijah Thrush for over ten days, during which time I read about their arrest in a large oversize newspaper, and their more recent release from jail. Both had their pictures in the paper, and both looked so inexpressibly ugly I wondered how I had ever been able to endure their company. Yet when one was in their presence, they seemed more lively than all the rest of the world put together, and young and beautiful in every way.

I felt both guilty and responsible toward Millicent and Elijah. I could not explain my emotions toward them or toward anybody. But just as my predicament which led me to my visits to the secret "chambers" in Wall Street had occupied a great deal of my time and energy, Millicent De Frayne and Elijah now began, if not to supersede my first "attachment" or "habit," to be very undeniably potent in my thoughts.

I went to her Fifth Avenue apartment, but the doorman insisted she had left the country. I told him a lie to the effect she had just that moment telephoned me, so, rather sheepish, he put me in the ivory-paneled elevator with the green cockatoo designs, and I went up to the second floor, falling almost over Norah as I alit.

"Miss De Frayne is not expecting you, Peggs," Norah recited, keeping the elevator door open so that I would get into it again and descend.

"I will not see deserters, traitors and impostors!" Millicent's voice rose, almost unrecognizable in rage. "Have him shown out. My check will be sent to him . . ."

I walked resolutely into the room from which the voice came. She was looking very bad from rheumatism, and had on a Paisley shawl, most unbecoming.

"I will not let you dispose of me as you did your other gentlemen retainers," I said and sat down on the tuffet with her.

"I suppose I am a pushover for brazenness in anybody," she said.

"I wish you would always wear your furs. A shawl don't bring out the harum-scarum in you . . ."

Before Millicent could reply, she became aware that Norah meanwhile was standing in the threshold of the receiving, or as she called it, her "withdrawing," room.

"You may go about your duties, Norah. Mr. Peggs has some talking to do . . ."

Her tongue-lashing of me now began. She accused me of every shortcoming, failure, misdeed, and meanness, so that I felt I was certainly related to her by blood. Only a mother could have been so cruel to me. I finally cried very hard, and it was a great pleasure and relief to both of us.

"I can never forgive that you did not go to jail with me. It was the least you could do, let us say."

I told her of the robber who had taken my clothing, exposing me, and explained that the police would have been very hard on me for this alone.

"Subterfuges, my dear, evasions."

A butler had brought her her furs, and she put some heavy white powder over her cheeks.

"I found another of the little notes which I presume you write to yourself," she said, after she had made herself more presentable, "and it touched me as much as your first note. If you could only get it out of your mind that I want your body! I want your body in heaven, not here . . . But to the note: here 'tis." She pulled out a heavy gilded lorgnette with cupids on one side, and read: "Though my meeting Millicent De Frayne and Elijah Thrush had set me apart from other men, my finally being admitted to the full grandeur and presence of these scintillating personages has ended my early life and career entirely, and ushered me into, well, into the something no man will ever describe."

"I have decided to kiss you on the mouth," she studied my lips with that angry attention I had seen only in doctors. "Come forward."

I kneeled between her two gray satin slippers, and she took my mouth in hers. Her tongue, resembling a cow's in roughness and vigor, explored the inside of my cheeks, tongue, and every single one of my teeth.

"You are in perfect health!" she said as she disengaged herself at last. "We will go on together, Albert. I had cashiered you, but because of your daring, I will retain you. I want you to betray Elijah, however, just as he has betrayed me. Please rise. Now leave the room."

 will not see that wretched turncoat, and you can go tell him to scat!" Elijah spoke to Eugene Belamy, who had announced me. "He's as false as water, a talebearer, tell him, Eugene, and any man's sweetmeat . . . Goes from one party to another, repeating this slander, heating up this old bit of calumny, wounding here, opening an old sore there, rubbing in salt down there, and always looking like an angelic little boy, though he claims maturity. Tell him to go back where his bread's buttered as thick as his finger . . . And I don't mean Alabama. And let old Millicent eat him alive for all I care . . ."

When Eugene reappeared in the room, I spoke to him in my stentor voice: "Tell Elijah I haven't the least intention of being driven out of here like a green grocer without first seeing him.

"I have had Elijah on my heart and mind ever since the disaster of the recital, tell him, but as a black youth, I could not run the risk of police apprehension, get him to understand . . ."

"You're no more black than I am, precious," Elijah's voice came nearer and nearer to where I was seated in my favorite chair. "You're the whitest smoothest thing I ever met."

The curtain drew back between the room where I sat and from where his voice had come. He seemed to be wearing a mask, for he was so decisively young-looking. He wore a crocus bathrobe, and had on gloves, in which as I was to learn later, there was almond meal to keep his hands and wrists free of wrinkles.

"You can fool everybody but Elijah," he told me, and sat down about a room apart from me. Eugene Belamy was seated also, on the piano stool, and began playing some Liszt, at sleepy tempo.

"I suppose, Albert, you're only interested in money, and yet there's something about you," he let his voice trail and then he rose, and came over to my chair, and picked up one hand, my left one, and then my right one, and studied them briefly, and then walked back to his chair, continuing to speak, "There's something in the whites of your eyes, especially, that tells me you're not all bad . . ."

"How grand you always are, Elijah Thrush," I snapped at him.

"I will not allow impertinence from someone who has already been shown the door," he flared up, but it was clear to me he was not seriously angry.

"That creature you work for is at least a hundred years old, I suppose you know that . . . If you weren't so unversed in the ways of her ilk I would tell you how she keeps her youth."

I half-closed my eyes, deliberately feigning lack of interest.

"Are you awake, my dear . . ."

"I think I know how she keeps her youth," I finally said.

"Well, indeed, then you're the first of her many ambassadors who's ever found out. But of course you're quite unusually, yes, egregiously clever . . ."

"She has nothing whatsoever to do, and hence her youth," I told him.

He laughed his Shakespearean madman laugh. "Idling is the one thing ages people the most. I once knew an heiress who was not even allowed to lift a book when she was reading. At thirty she looked ninety . . . No, you're on the wrong tack, Albert, my dear, you couldn't be further askew . . .

"Her only passion, to go back to Millicent De Frayne, to go back always to her, for she has pursued me since 1913, as you are tired of hearing by now! Her only interest, aim, or program is to look exactly as she did, in that antediluvian year. She early in her career discovered how to keep her youth. It has aged her as much, however, as it has kept her green. However, somehow, whether it's the earliness of the hour, or your own childish mentality, I cannot bring myself to tell you . . ."

"I have never liked being coaxed. It sometimes brings on fits of great anger," I warned, and I stretched out my chest and arms, to remind him of my strength.

"You have noticed," he went on after studying what I believe was my feet, for they are quite large, and one of my early admirers said such long narrow feet prevented my being an Adonis, "you have of course noticed since you are admitted to her castle nearly daily, that there is always a file of extremely young men in waiting on her. By that I mean they are waiting to see her . . ."

"I have noticed quite a number of waiting boys, true," I spoke in a manner bordering on gravity.

"Well, draw your own conclusions, damn it! I'll say no more." He looked at a huge gold watch, which he had withdrawn from his crocus bathrobe.

"I never think of her as having lovers," I said. "Though she pets me occasionally."

"Oh, that only means she's not serious about your body," he replied in a tone meant to comfort me. "No, there's no need to go on, Albert, for I can't tell you." He now rose.

"Eugene, that's quite enough of Franz Liszt, you may

retire," the Mime scolded the piano player, then sighed heavily three times.

"Since you are forcing me to tell you, I will, but not with any details," he went on, once the pianist had retired. "I realize that you probably wish to know the secret of her unusual youth for the pure professional reasons that you are her ambassador . . ."

"Spy," I corrected him.

He smiled very acidly.

Then going up to me and putting both his arms on my shoulders, he looked into the healthy whites of my eyes, and said, "She does not love these young men. She does not love anybody. But in order to preserve her youth"—and here he turned away from me, letting out great cries of vexation and loathing, impatience and anger with, I suppose, the makeup of the world in general— "that horrible creature extracts their semen with a siphon, one extract after another from those perfect specimens of youth, without tenderness, interest in their bodies—or minds—as coldly and as calculatedly as a surgeon, dismissing them afterwards with a huge sum of money, never to see them again . . . Don't you see the creature is an enemy to all that love means to us? She's a monster. It's not right of God to let her rove free . . ."

The snow, after having thrilled me, began to freeze my Alabama blood and constitution. All I could do was drink gunpowder tea and remain for as long as was decent in the dining room of the Divine Fairgroves Hotel, where one gusty evening who should be introduced to me there by Amanda Duddell but the piano player from the Arcturus Gardens, his overshoes looking like snowdrifts, and his scarf dripping with icicles.

I was too astonished even to bid him sit down, and he fell heavily into an armchair.

"You will have to overlook my barging in on you, Mr. Peggs," he began.

"I hope you don't bring bad news from Elijah Thrush!"

"There's nothing wrong with Elijah Thrush; there never is, is there? It's what's wrong with me that brings me clear over here," and as he said this he rolled his head about as if he had got to China.

"This is my home away from Alabama," I spoke in a falsetto. "Can Amanda bring you some refreshment . . ." She was standing by my left hand, and immediately took out a little pad and a pencil and waited for Eugene Belamy's instructions.

"I suppose you must have spoon bread," he spoke loftily.

Amanda indicated by facial gesture that they had none, and would not be having any in the near future.

"Oh, just bring any of your typical desserts then," he commanded her.

After an awkward pause which I was unable to break, and during which he had divested himself of his overcoat, and one of the doormen had placed newspapers under his dripping feet, Amanda brought him a semolina pudding, with two cherries on top, which he dispiritedly toyed with.

"I may as well come to the point at once, Mr. Peggs, for I have no art of diplomacy, and my heart is broken . . . You must give up Elijah Thrush. There are no two ways about it. My own happiness, my very sanity is at stake, not to mention my bread and butter . . ." He pushed his pudding aside with such force the plate hovered perilously on the edge of the table.

"It is a rule of the house that diners must finish all that they order," I spoke to him confidentially. "Not a scrap or morsel must go back to the kitchen without an explanation. It would create a very touchy situation."

Eugene Belamy went quite pale. He was, now I had time to study him, indeed a very handsome young man, with ringlets of gold, fresh complexion, strong chin, but a very tiny buttonhole mouth, which prevented him from being an Apollo. His long black eyelashes, however, must have won him many admirers among a special clientele. His hands rather shocked me for those of a piano player, for they were on the short and stubby side, and looked as if he had washed a great many dishes, in piping hot suds.

While I had been studying his good looks he had wolfed down all the semolina pudding and banged the spoon into the plate.

"Would he like more?" Amanda inquired of me.

"Would you, Eugene?" I said with strong coaxing expression in my voice.

"Nothing more, unless you have a finger bowl."

Amanda and I both shook our heads.

"I'll freshen up in your room, then, Mr. Peggs," he told me.

"That won't be possible," I said as I exchanged a look with Amanda Duddell. "The Divine Fairgroves Hotel does not allow visitors in the rooms, unless by special permission of Father Divine. But we have a fine consulting room." I waved my arm toward a pleasant green room with heavy chairs, and soft lights.

"It will have to do, I suppose." He rose. "The main thing is intimacy and not being overheard."

We sat at a mammoth walnut table on which stood a little green-shaded lamp, and Eugene began drumming his fingers on the wood. His breath caused a kind of clouding on the wood's surface, and he would take out his handkerchief then and rub over the clouded portion.

"Peggs, you must give up Elijah, as I said earlier. You have everything. I have nothing. Nothing but Elijah."

"I can't very well give up what I don't have." I tightened my necktie.

"I beg your pardon," he said, but his attention had become fixed suddenly on an old upright piano.

"I don't belong to Elijah Thrush," I told him, "or he to me. You surely know . . ."

"But Elijah is completely smitten with you . . . If you could play the piano, I would be turned out of his studio tonight, and so out of his life . . ." He studied my hands. "You don't play of course. But don't you see, if you would only go away, back to Alabama, my life could continue the way it is, and you would not miss him in any case . . . It's only infatuation on your part. With me it's a way of life, a life style, as the vulgar daily press calls it. I cannot go on without Elijah Thrush. You, on the other hand, are in demand everywhere. It is your period."

"Oh, this will never do," I grumbled, trying to control my anger.

"You have Millicent De Frayne, if you don't want to go home to Alabama."

"But the only reason I have her is to . . . well, spy on Mr. Thrush. The two go together. Surely you must see that."

Eugene Belamy now took out a violet envelope marked in large black handwriting FOR ALBERT PEGGS, ESQUIRE.

"Please take it," he said as I hesitated.

I opened it and peeked within. As I more or less foresaw, it was a thousand-dollar bill.

"All I ask is that you go away," the piano player spoke sobbing.

I put the money in my breast pocket.

"You know I cannot go anywhere," I said. "I'm very sorry. I'm under contract, as it were . . ."

"I'll give you anything," he began, weeping hard. "You can use me any way you like. I know you have a very expensive habit, that is why I have given you this money. Perhaps you beat people. I am willing to have you beat me and abuse me in the current fashion, if this is your pleasure."

"The smell of blood is not my repertoire . . ."

"But your habit, Mr. Peggs . . . Don't you see it will destroy you? Why not take my money and go to Alabama . . ."

"Do you wish your money back?" I took the envelope out of my breast pocket, and offered it to him.

"Of course not. That never crossed my mind . . ."

He sniffed very hard.

"Here I offer you everything, my body, my entire fortune, my all, and what do I get. Insults and contumely from a . . . a . . ."

"Ripe eggplant, Eugene," I said. "Now *you* see here. I am just as smitten with Elijah Thrush as you are. Why I don't know. There's everything wrong with him—"

"I'll tell him—" interposed Eugene.

"—everything askew and a-lop, and all that, and he can't dance or sing anymore, and his poems are not right, but all I know is the minute I see him, I am in paradise, seventh heaven, Turkish delight, Nirvana, and total sensual and mental pleasure . . . He sets me off like four hundred

tops, and I won't stop for a wedding cake figurine like
yourself. Why can't I have the same pleasures in life as
you? And so what if I am a spy. You look up to me as
a black man of course, but that ain't my ticket."

I rose then and bent down and kissed him on the mouth
to make my contract and agreement with him sure and
binding.

I have a scrapbook which contains within its pages
under a protective kind of isinglass all the wild flowers
and some of the leaves of the trees of my native state of
Alabama. During these depressed periods of my life, such
as that after my interview with Eugene Belamy, I would
retire to the library of the Divine Fairgroves Hotel, and
look at my scrapbook. I hardly noticed the falling snow
outside, or the sad black faces of those around me, who,
having chosen New York as their goal, had lost everything they had ever been before.

I had already gotten by heart the "faces" and names of
my favorite wild flowers, but tonight, after my meeting
with Eugene Belamy, I kissed each flower gently as I
renewed its name: shortspur columbine, thimbleberry, rue
anemone, nodding ladies' tresses, heart-leafed twayblade,
and chickasaw plum.

My nostrils were again greedily taking in the perfume
from these flowers, unknown in New York, when Ros-
coe George shook me gently by the shoulder and, bowing
in his capacity as doorman, told me I was wanted on the
"outside" telephone.

"Where in God's name have you been, when I am in
such earnest need of you?" Elijah's voice thundered over
the wire, as actual as if he had been sitting in the Divine
Fairgroves Hotel. "Answer me . . ."

"Waylaid by your piano player!" I shouted back, dis-

turbing several ladies who were slumbering in the Peach
Room, hard by.

"I am ruined," Elijah went on, not having heard possibly
my mention of Belamy's visit . . . "It's all over, my dear.
The wicked creature with the ten fortunes has won her
legal battle and now has taken custody of my great-grandson—known as the Bird of Heaven, you recall, by his
intimates. This is her final card to bring me to my knees
. . . All is over, all is . . ."

Somehow, to my own stupefaction, I had hung up. I
walked back into the library, after having given a bow
here and there to the seated ladies in the Peach Room, and
slumped down on the davenport. I had done it now, hung
up on the Mime, which was an offense as terrible as having
slobbered on the outstretched hand of royalty. I was
through. New York was over. I was glad, yet I was
terrified. No, he would never forgive me.

Then my attention dreamily wandered back to what
he had said. His great-grandson, about whom he had
talked so often, was a prisoner of Millicent De Frayne.

Despite my having overheard the Mime's interview with
his great-grandson before the barred window of the Alimentary Foundation, I still doubted the Bird of Heaven
existed. I thought it was just a way of speaking . . . An
ideal love, divine paederasty, about which he talked so
much, Plato with his beloved disciples, Jesus, with his, etc.
But the great-grandson existed.

I rubbed my eyes, and looked out at the snow. Yes,
it was white, and it was real, and it was falling, I need
not pinch myself, and Alabama was thousands of miles,
far far off, and back there everybody was dead, or
those who had remained had forgotten me, and here a
white man Eugene had kneeled to me, had offered me

his body to do with as I pleased, which I had courteously declined, and the next day Millicent De Frayne would be waiting in her withdrawing room to give me new instructions. Suddenly I put my wrist to my ear and listened. It beat on, poor confused heart, pumping away, not knowing any better, when there was so little to pump for. I closed the book of wild flowers. While pressing my wrist to my ear, I had caught the smell of my own perspiration; it was quite different, let the truth be told, from Millicent De Frayne's or Elijah's, but on the whole, I thought, more agreeable to a universal sense of smell.

Stop! Eyes only for the President!" Millicent De Frayne's voice boomed as I was about to go into her withdrawing room. This incomprehensible remark, however, did not make me hesitate, but I walked directly into her presence. "Eyes only for the . . ." she had begun again, but my own cries of astonishment drowned out her repetition of the sentence.

I cannot say that I was astonished at what I saw, because astonishment had begun to disappear from my makeup; still I was taken aback, because I was unprepared for this particular spectacle in her big room. For one thing, Millicent was standing without her cane or any other support. The big surprise of course was that directly in front of her, kneeling, was the Mime himself. There was nothing penitent, however, or servile, in his expression, and he looked, indeed, as though *he* was standing over a cowering Millicent De Frayne.

"I might have known you would come in at such

a moment!" he shrieked at me. "You have no sense of timing, my sweet. I'm afraid I am tiring of you . . ."

"That would be a hard blow to get over, Elijah," I told him, and I did not speak with irony. I meant what I said.

"How touching a remark, Elijah," Millicent spoke from her great height, and, she was, have I remembered to emphasize, standing or sitting a very tall person: I believe she must have been six feet in her stocking soles.

"I don't know why I am always being seen at my worst by people who have not had a proper introduction to my life and my work. I must give him my unpublished autobiography, Millicent, pray remind me, and the privately published book of poems and aphorisms . . ."

"I wish you would either rise, my dear, or let me call for assistance from one of my staff . . ."

"Count on you, my dear, to speak like a parcel of jackasses," the Mime cried as he began to advance on his knees toward a large sacristy cabinet, in which instead of priestly vestments Millicent kept a small collection of monocles, and some wine and medicines.

"I don't know why, but humiliation is one aspect of reality I could never get used to," Elijah cried, and at that moment I realized somehow what his predicament was: he had slipped and fallen, and owing to his age and condition of his bones, he was unable to rise.

"Allow me, dear Elijah," I went toward him.

"Yes, yes, allow the dear boy!" Millicent cried.

"Stand back, and away, you idiots!" Elijah cried, and although his face went purple from the exertion, and a looking glass or two and a notebook fell out from his inner clothing, he did manage, by holding on to the sacristy cabinet to get up on one leg, and then, disobeying him, I helped him rise on the other.

"Perfectly grand, perfectly wonderful! Hosanna indeed!" Millicent cried.

I picked up the looking glasses, and the notebook, and began looking through the latter before I was conscious of my bad manners. Millicent, seeing what I was doing, said in a low voice, "Try to memorize aught you see there, Albert."

"I don't know which of us ought to explain to Mr. Peggs what the occasion of my being here is," Elijah began after he was in one of Millicent's more ample stick-back chairs, and I had reached him back his papers. "I am, however, and let this be put down in writing, if you wish, for it seems to be the end of everything, I'm capitulating. I've just learned, through this big fat newspaper, that she's succeeded in adopting the Bird of Heaven, otherwise known as my great-grandson . . ."

Millicent was studying the rib of an old parasol which she herself had been mending, for as she told me on another occasion, there were no umbrella menders now alive, the last one, a charming Viennese man, a bare four feet eleven, had just emigrated, leaving nobody to do her repairs.

"All I have done, dear Mime, is to take out papers for the boy's adoption, and immediately Elijah," she appealed to me, "feels that I am harboring the boy in this already too crowded apartment."

At that moment, however, we heard a child's laughter, and a man dressed in chauffeur's costume came through an adjoining room, with a young chap in an Indian suit, and long black curls.

The Mime shaded his eyes, and even Millicent looked somewhat discomfited.

The boy disentangled his hand from the chauffeur and

went over to the chair where his great-grandfather was sitting.

"Long ago," Elijah said, without taking his hands away from his eyes, "as far back as the teens of this century I got rid of the critics by simply entering a world where they could not enter, and about which, for all their tacky cleverness, they could not gain one scrap of information. But this harpy, who has pursued me through the lifetime of several men, can walk through iron doors and concrete to get at me . . . Now she has taken my only love away from me!"

"You neglected him, honeybunch."

Then without a warning of any kind, issuing from the great-grandson came a cascade of the most sylvan sounds which perhaps have ever issued from human lips. I felt a thrill of some indefinable kind, as if I had been transported to some earlier half-human existence of my own thousands upon thousands of years before. The boy stood there, a mute, but from his lips just the same one heard a forest of singing birds, a talent and power of which he had given no indication as he had stood behind the bars of the Alimentary Foundation.

I noticed that even Millicent De Frayne was listening attentively, with closed eyes, to these sounds of nature, but the boy's performance was too much for the Mime. He bowed his head, and from his eyes a thin stream of tears descended like tiny pieces of plaster falling from a broken wall.

"Don't you see, Albert," he spoke as if in prayer, "this criminal sneak has succeeded at last in bringing me to heel! By keeping the Bird here prisoner, she has me also as good as under lock and key."

"Medieval rubbish, and you know it, Elijah!" Millicent

scoffed. "We can all live happily together, like larks, if only we will. But the meaning of life, my cherub, is concession."

"She talks of concession who never gave one in her life," the Mime spoke through a series of tuneless laughs. "Compromise, concession, admission, yielding—simpering commonplaces she despises in her own heart . . ."

While Elijah went on fulminating against her, Millicent had persuaded the Bird to sit upon her lap and was ceremoniously giving his lips silent kisses, and after each kiss she would repeat, "Bluer than claret and much bluer than cherry!" Whether she was describing the fetching color of the boy's mouth, or singing another of her old ballads, nobody could be sure.

*W*ell, my dear Albert, you see the postulant to-day raised from the floor, it is true, but he is still on his knees, in any practical sense, and may remain there forever."

Elijah Thrush was speaking to me in the room behind his theater stage, and I was here, at his command, to attend a dress rehearsal of his next public performance.

He looked as composed as I suppose he could in view of the fact that Millicent had taken his great-grandson from the general security of the Alimentary Foundation and was now keeping him, in the Mime's words, "under house arrest" in her own sumptuous suite.

Elijah sat on one of his sgabello chairs, for he preferred an uncomfortable seat when he was about to give out un-pleasant or important information, which was the case now. In his left hand, a telegram, opened, was waving in the breeze which came from a broken window through which some stray gray pigeons had entered expecting sunflower seeds.

"She communicates damnable messages like this through the public channels," he pushed the telegram under my eyes. I read:

CONSOLE YOURSELF. ALL OWL EGGS ARE WHITE.
MILLICENT.

"Can you make a thing out of it?" He came near to laughing. "Had she sent it to you, I would take it to be an example of her superiority, her being a firm believer in endogamy. Mark my words, all her interest in you is mere infatuation with the exotic, plus the fact that your prestige as a black is now higher than that of some white Apollo whom she might employ for spying on me . . .

"But let me tell you how she is attempting to win the boy away from me, who am the only one in the world he loves, and the only one whom I love, though I care for you deeply, Albert, but I don't think you quite appreciate my own great qualities. But hear now how that rip on a broomstick is proceeding to win him away from me.

"First of all she has called in several orchestras of trombones and saxophones to play for him, as like most young people of today he is more at home with sounds than with words . . . When the orchestras are not amusing him, he has the palmarium, you know, where under huge tropical date palms and amid giant cacti a chorus of selected parrots, specially trained, call to the boy in different languages, praising him, and comforting his loneliness, *and*, don't let your attention stray here, my fetching friend, each parrot has been taught oh with such fiendish finesse to denigrate, malign, and utterly destroy my character . . ."

The Mime was wearing his famous "spotted" ermine, a dilapidated garment, which as a matter of fact Millicent herself had bestowed on him, many many seasons past, and he tugged at it savagely as he spoke.

"Today is rehearsal day," the Mime spoke now in a less aggrieved tone, "and Eugene should be here almost any moment . . . I do wish you would stay and tell me which of the numbers we will go through are in your opinion the most effective. But I want you to engrave on the chambers of your heart that Millicent, whose bread you eat, though I forgive you for it, for I understand shame and poverty, especially when they go together, as they always I suspect do, engrave on your heart the terrible knowledge that she believes only in endogamy. Her love for you is specious."

At this moment a surly uncombed Eugene Belamy entered the room, with a sheaf of music in one hand, and his lunch in the other.

"*You're* from the country, Eugene," the Mime's voice followed me as I went into the next room to wait for the performance, "what color do you think owl eggs are . . ."

Was this only a rehearsal for a coming Sunday I was attending, I began to muse, looking about me, or had I sunk, through all my bad luck, at last to some underground kingdom to become as insubstantial and incomprehensible as all those who sat beside me, for lo and behold there was now not a vacant spot in the house, and the young assistant to Eugene Belamy, Fred Firminger, in the unexplained absence of Mother Macaulay and her black satin gown, had suddenly appeared in major-domo costume in order to place on the tiny stage, as in old-time vaudeville, a whopping red sign whose gray letters read:

NUMBER FOUR OF THE SUNDAY REPERTORY,
"FORBIDDEN MEMORIES"
INTERPRETED BY THE WORLD-FAMOUS MIME,
STAR OF STAGE & SILVER SCREEN,
WHO APPEARED IN THE ORIGINAL FILM "BEN-HUR"
AND MADE HIS DEBUT
ON THE STEPS OF THE PARTHENON:
THE ETERNAL ELIJAH THRUSH!

Every hand in the house was clapping violently when Fred Firminger again appeared, and this time instead of beating the gong, as Mother Macaulay always did on Sundays, to announce the beginning of the performance, he blew through an immense conch shell, making a sound which was so effective and haunting that the Mime told me later that he had decided the moment he heard it that from now on forwards he would replace the old Chinese gong with the ocean shell, for he felt the latter was more consonant with his pagan background.

From the wings now one could hear the Mime reciting lines from the Greek Anthology, in his inimitable tomb-like voice, and then he surprised us by leaping without the least warning, almost like an athlete, to the very front of the stage, whose papery boards gave back creaking echoes. Then coming to a full halt before the footlights, with closed painted eyelids, he let his admirers feast upon his face, with the great rident smile of carmined lips, his hat, which resembled a large sewing basket, and his four strings of beads, beneath which he wore only a cache-sexe.

Ancient as Elijah was, with his old sinews, and droop-
ing pectorals, and a generous accretion of suet around
his navel, as he waved his arms in time to the sugary
music coming from the upright piano, he let me see back-
wards some fifty or sixty years the young man he may
have been, wooing tired Parisian audiences with his fron-
tier vigor and naïveté, and I was sinking back into this
wonderful reverie, when a hand threw a note in my
lap, and the spell was broken. I think the Mime sensed
this, for he stopped in his dance, and looked me full in
the face, interrupting a movement, and then with a frown
which aged him considerably and a sneer on his mouth
which did nothing for his beauty, he threw himself
again into the fury of his dance, his beads twirling and
striking against one another. I looked down at my lap,
at the letter. I opened it to the wide orange penciled
words:

THE MIME CALLS YOU TARBOX THE SUPERB BEHIND YOUR BACK:
CHEW ON THAT FOR A COMPLIMENT, SWELL-HIDE!

The attempted cruelty of the note, through an expression long well known to me, so unstrung me that I advanced without my knowing I was doing so directly onto
the little stage, where one of his long strings of beads
struck me full in the face with such force that it drew
blood, and I believe, though it all remains confused, this
blood was thrown back upon the Mime's body. He was
in a vaulting fury, however, when he saw me on the
stage, waving my paper at him, and crying out, as I
always do, when moved, in falsetto, so that later I realized
I had sounded like the darky in a minstrel show, as I
said, "Did you abuse me by calling me this behind my
back, sir?" and so unusual was my question, not to speak
of my presence on stage, he took one look at the paper,

and saw the word. He had his lips set to say something, when the door was thrown open, and there stood Millicent De Frayne, with her hand on the head of the Bird of Heaven, who was dressed like his great-granddaddy, in flowing toga-like robes, a garland on his head, and sandals. In his one free hand, for the other clasped that of Millicent, he held a bouquet of anemones.

"You see how clever, ladies and gentlemen, this pit viper is," and then turning to Eugene Belamy he cried, "Stop banging the keys, Mr. Nonesuch, for God's sake, can't you see the entire rehearsal is ruined by that money-bags and these two poor simpletons who are in her pay—" and he moved his head in the direction of me and his great-grandson.

"But this terrible pejorative must be explained, Elijah Thrush," I cried.

"Why don't you open at least one eye to daylight?" he addressed me in a cold fury. "This letter was written and dispatched to you by your employer, the noted seducer of youths under twenty, Millicent Charbonneau De Frayne, or by one of her countless accomplices . . ."

Millicent and the boy were already on the stage, and I saw indeed how small it was now, for there was just about room for the four of us. She read the note briefly without her lorgnette, and then turned to me. "It's the Mime's handwriting, my dear Albert. The whole world knows he's a bigot."

"I came here, ladies and gentlemen," Millicent addressed the audience, and a more attentive one never filled seats, "because I am the last woman in the world to keep blood kin asunder . . . Harkee," she bent over the blinking footlights, "you are my witnesses. I came here most gentlewomanly with his darling great-grandson, who suffers under an affliction, the sweetheart is dumb from birth, though perfect in every other part of his body," and Millicent bent to kiss him on the mouth, "but this elder Adonis of the stage and screen has never shown the slightest interest in the boy . . . He was about, this priceless lad was, to be put in a county home for the defective. I intervened . . ."

"You intervened, Charbonneau, for one and one purpose only . . . Ladies and gentlemen," Elijah spoke sotto voce to the audience, "let me tell you how this creature here with her billions of fortune, keeps her youth, for she's over a hundred if she's a minute . . . I intend to speak the whole truth here today . . . Let me . . ."

"I demand to know, sir, if you have ever called me a Superb Tarbox," I now thundered to Elijah, pulling him in my distraction by all pairs of his black beads.

"Yes, I did," he replied coolly, "and I'm not sorry. What's wrong with calling you by the color you came from your mother's body as, answer me that. One minute you want me to praise your shoe-black ass, and the next I'm to speak of you as a field of alabaster lilies. You can't have it both ways. You're black as midnight and why shouldn't I as the greatest plastic artist of the body living today so denominate you. Why should I grovel to the fads and whims of the present epoch!"

I descended the few steps leading away from the stage. On the bottom step was an old top hat which was to be used in a later number. I had long fancied it, and I took it up and put it on my head.

I stood there not moving a muscle for a long time, and one could have heard a pin drop.

Then I slowly unbuttoned, and took out my much-prized member. I think I did this in the correct style, it was funereal, slow and perfectly timed. Then bowing

to each and every person in the audience, I beat my
retreat into the hall.

Once outside, however, I began to cry, as I adjusted
my clothing.

As I was going down the staircase, for I didn't want
to wait for the elevator, I heard the Mime's voice calling,
"Albert! For God in heaven's sake, come back, my darling.
Come back, for sweet heaven's sake, come back . . ."

𝒫 ray, don't loiter and idle outside, as though you had
no business in the house, you're on the roster after all,
good land, and so come in, my only, for you look more
alarmed than I am ill, do enter, do." Millicent spoke to
me from her "field bed," though I had always thought
until she told me so that such a bed was a four-poster,
with a canopy, and all, but she insisted on field bed,
and told me it was at least two hundred and fifty years old.

"Dr. Hitchmough is just leaving, Albert," she exclaimed,
clearing her throat and then nodding to a very elderly-
looking man with a goat beard and glasses with ribbons
dangling from them.

"Who is this dusky young person?" the doctor almost
cried out as he examined me very closely.

"A memoirist, Dr. Hitchmough, a memoirist."

"Of what, my dear Millicent, may I inquire?"

"Haven't you asked a good too many questions already
of a woman you have diagnosed as very very tired . . ."

"Corrected as always by one of my own patients!" He
shook his head several times and gave out a convulsive

cough-like laugh. "But pray don't worry about your ovaries any more, my dear," he said.

"I certainly won't for I never have."

"I wish many a girl of eighteen had ovaries as fine as yours, Millicent."

"Well, don't be too generous! Wishing gifts away is not my manner of doing things at all, Hitchmough. Never was, and 'twon't be. It's one's hereditary stock that's the ticket, and you know it better than I. Your absurd praise of democracy and charity has led you astray professionally again and again."

"My dear, you always run ahead of my argument."

"I won't have my best parts being wished off on hoi polloi . . . Albert and I here have had a great many humiliations lately and I wonder he is up and around, though I see—come closer, my pet—he's been clawed, it looks like by a wild animal . . . Oh, youth, Doctor Hitchmough, youth has no fear of the cosmos . . ."

Millicent now examined my face very closely, and touched the scratches and claw marks finally with a bit of her spit.

"Pray have a look at Albert, Dr. Hitchmough, you won't charge anything extra, will you, for he's part of the household . . . Do, doctor, take him over to the daylight there and have a good deep look. There!"

Dr. Hitchmough led me over to the huge bay window, and gazed into my face, and eyes.

"Are you a sporting man?" he spoke in a voice loud enough to reach Millicent.

"Just diagnose, why don't you, Hitchmough, my love, don't go into his history like that. He's from Alabama. I may visit it, for he's told me perfectly exotic marvels about it."

"He's been scratched by some large bird, I fancy . . ."

"Well, prescribe something for him, in your wisdom, some little pill or liquid, for Albert and I must be busy today. He's done me no end of good, Dr. Hitchmough, you've no idea . . ."

The doctor wrote out something hurriedly.

"Pray pass that to Jordan, the butler, on the way out and he'll fill it," he addressed me icily, as he sealed the prescription in an envelope.

"*You* have absolutely no cause for alarm, my dear," Dr. Hitchmough whinnied, bent over his patient, and kissed her on the mouth. "And don't ever again blame it on your ovaries . . . And don't forget the ounce of raw chopped meat before bedtime. 'Twill make a big difference, Millicent."

"Off with you then, doctor, for we've so much to do, Albert and I. He's not ill, then, you say . . . Oh, wonderful, for I couldn't accompany him back to Alabama should he prove invalid, and I can't lose him now, after all I've put out for him."

The moment Dr. Hitchmough left, Millicent De Frayne leaped up from bed with the alacrity of a young man, put on her house slippers, and went over to a Trafalgar upright chair, and fairly spat out the words, "Charlatans all of them, Albert, yet we never know when we're feeling a bit down we may have some fatal bug that will put us under the sod . . . Did you get a glimpse at all of the paper he wrote out for you, for you're awfully good at reading things that pass under your eyes . . ."

"I have come to tell you goodbye, Millicent, ma'am," I told her. "I can't stand it."

"What is it?" she said.

"All of it."

"Me, you mean," she said.

Like lightning she moved to a mahogany card table with splayfeet, and from a drawer inside took out a gun, which she leveled at me.

"Now tell me what it was you said," she cried. "And don't think I don't mean business. If I shoot you, there'll be nobody to know it, except maybe you, but 'twill be too quick for you to really understand until you're flying in heaven. I suppose you believe in heaven . . ."

"Oh, I toy with the idea."

"I'd as soon kill you as kiss you," she said. She put the gun back in the drawer.

"You understand the Mime of Tenth Avenue," she mused. "Why and how I don't know. My white memoirists never understood a thing about him. They either pitied him, the Christians, or they wanted him to go on poor relief, the Jews. Love and justice, you know, both usually specious emotions. But you, my dear, are within all things. I can't lose you. I may kill you but I won't give you up . . . Now come here and kiss me, for even though your cheeks are bleeding you've never looked so tomato-ripe and pretty and oh such wavy hair and solemn eyebrows!"

My habit was turning against me, as witness the bruises, contusions, scratches, and hemorrhages all over my body, and what was worse, I realized that I had fallen hopelessly under the spell of Millicent and Elijah, and that it could only be described, improbable as it was, as the passion of love. They were replacing my habit in intensity, romance, and late-hour musings. They knew this, and their own natural cruelty, tyranny, and impossible demands were bulwarked and fortified by my falling for them. Henceforward they would be restrained in nothing, where it touched me, and I, "poor black pawn" in their game, would only yield to whatever indignity and outrage they might think up next. I had often thought of killing both of them, and now I had learned that at least one of them, Millicent, considered killing me. Elijah, needless to say, frequently told me he wished I was dead when I crossed him, which was almost continuous.

In my despair, I decided to disobey the command of Millicent and perhaps Elijah and visit the Bird of Heaven in his palmarium. He was at play as I entered the rather overheated, overbright room, the size of a large tennis court, and of course did not hear me enter since he was, in addition to being mute, slightly hard of hearing. He was arranging a row of turtles in preparation for a race they were to have. I touched him on his ringlets, and he slowly turned about and stared at me. He made a motion that I was to bend down, and he then touched my face assiduously, looking each time he touched at his hands and fingers. He touched me all over my face and hands, again, each time, looking at his own hands where they had touched me. At last he went to a pool of water, and brought back a small cup, and began washing my face industriously. I explained to him by gestures and words that my complexion would not come off, no matter what he or I did. I recalled then having heard from the Mime that the best way to communicate with the boy was by a sort of kissing sound, two kisses meant yes, and one kiss meant no. I also discovered then he heard very well what one said when he was addressed directly. He could only reply however by making the kissing sounds yes and no.

Again whether it was the many gifts which my habit had conferred on me or, in the words of Millicent De Frayne, "my Alabama charm," I found that the Bird of Heaven, after the surprise of discovering that my face did not rub off, became deeply attached to me, and I had the greatest difficulty leaving him, without his bursting into tears. It was me who also took the boy to the telephone and allowed him to call his great-grandfather, who would ask the boy a question, and the boy would reply either yes or no with a kissing sound.

I knew of course that Millicent was watching all this from some central compartment, where she had a sort of electronic eye which let her spy on the servants in whatever room they were (it was one of the reasons why the servants left either immediately or, blackmailed by her knowledge of what they did in their rooms, remained with her until old age handed them automatically over to the government and out of her house).

So my attachment, not counting my habit, which as I said was failing me, was three, the Bird of Heaven, Millicent, and the Mime of Tenth Avenue. But as each demanded to the full of my personality, my health continued to decline, though as I believe I said elsewhere, I became somehow at the same time younger-looking and stronger. Perhaps Love itself was devouring me, as it returned me to a strange boyhood.

Like the droppings from immense prehistoric birds, but white as the Northern snowfall, my notes, which were commissioned to be about Elijah Thrush but were incoherently divergently about everything, fell from my own clothing. Although Millicent De Frayne had examined my body in detail, marveling at its variegated color, not at all like the chocolate pie she had assumed it would be, but more like certain half-active lava beds, here a touch of coral color, there a laughing kind of pink, and beneath, angry earth tints, it was just as Elijah had forewarned me, her appetite was only satisfied with the youths, under twenty years of age, paid attendants, and the elixir from their bodies alone interested her, for in the task of extracting their manly milk, she had barely time to inspect their sundry beauties, or their spring charm.

But the pieces of paper on which I had written my reflections drove her first to a maniacal anger, and then this having subsided, and no medicine, either from the young men's finest parts, or from Dr. Hitchmough's medicine bag being able to help her, she sank into a black bile, and barely stirred from her chair beside her teapoy from which she helped herself to countless cups of gunpowder.

"Has he told the truth, this inky memoirist?" was her constant complaint, and then remembering this was only a word whilst the kaleidoscope of the deceived retina went on and on, until the eye itself ceased to take pictures, rotted with maggots and from maggots flown into fine dust, she commanded me to take my post.

"His biography," she said, meaning of course Elijah Thrush, "does not add up to even the thinnest sliced kind of doctrine! I mean reality, I suppose. What do I mean? You have fallen under his spell, as all do, you see him as a beautiful young man, which was the intention, you acknowledge my passion for him which knows no time, and yet, confound you, you have deceived me, as he has! I should flay you, for the reality of the body is deep deep under the skin, in those parts which are ever wet, laved by the lymph and blood and running matter which is the body's only life, and all the outside, my dear, which you and I feast on, is mere death and role-playing . . . What are we in love with? I must warn you,

Albert, your own presence is becoming so strong, the stench of your perfume has worked my nostrils into such a state of overactivity, you are a diet for me which may prove a poison supper at last . . . These notes," she brought them up from a kind of carpetbag which she had lying on the floor, and which scintillated like sapphires, "all are too unbearable. I will never have nightmares again, because I don't sleep. All that allows me to breathe, I fancy, is that you are suffering as much as I am. That is as it should be, and I have of course hired you with this certain thought in mind.

"That you would win over the love of the Bird of Heaven away from me is also exactly as I had foreseen, and yet once it is a fait accompli, I find the contingency unbearable. Why don't you kill me, and have done with it? Our only task, of course, remains, to grind Elijah Thrush to powder. We roll up our sleeves for this because it can't be done. But you must try harder, Albert. Bait him, confuse him, make love to him, pour out all the overripe richness of you which sickens and appetizes me, and of course continue to write these blackmail notes, since you are incapable of being a full-blown memoirist. You are incapable, you black whore, of being anything but you, wonderful, only *you* . . ."

She commanded me now to kiss her, and as she did so she tore badly my newest pongee shirt, so that indeed, seeing myself in her pier mirror, I looked like one who had been flayed.

"I know what your habit is," she accused as she leveled a look at me. "You can thank God I do." She wiped my saliva from her mouth. "Few women can plunge downward as far as I, and yet come up so happy and light, putting any dolphin to shame. Now get to him, and make his life the hell he has made mine, do you hear, Bought-and-Paid-for . . ."

I fell at her feet in a seizure of the most pronounced kind in my memory. She listened to my weeping with the fine attention and critical detachment of the perfect eardrum made by God for this moment, and no other. From before the creation it had been destined I would cry like this, in tones so piteous any other ear than hers would have been pierced. There had never been anyone, for as I say, it was destiny, who would understand the cries, and then the little streamlets of blood which came from my nose. They were beyond ecstasy for her, and made our relationship impossible of severance.

"Plant any seed you like in his mind, sweetest Albert," she whispered as she put something into my hand, "make my presence weigh on him wherever his hand or eye move. I don't want him to know a minute's respite now, for we're out of time, and let the Bird of Heaven talk to him by the hour on the phone. He can't ever have him anyhow unless he has me, and that's how we've won this victory, which, my angel, is so complete, I would have to say, if I were another woman, it is killing me . . . Open that other door to the jonquil room, as you go out, some young gentleman is waiting to see me out there . . ."

"Come, hither, my cherub," Millicent De Frayne spoke to the Bird of Heaven as he came hesitant but not cringing into her withdrawing room. She took the boy's hand in hers.

"You are like a diadem of stars after the presence of that black jaguar whose sleek movements leave me all throbs. My mouth is full of musk from his kisses . . . Would you believe it, my dearest of wards, that I once looked out on the world in the cloudless blue I see in your eyes. I too expected something, but, if I may be allowed some frankness, your blue is already clouding. Blame me for it, if you like. I expect to be blamed. Sit on the tabouret, sparrow, and let me toy with your ringlets. You fear me, but I will never harm you." She brought him closer to her knees, and he let his head fall against them as if an invisible sword had severed it.

"I have something I have found by and large better than love, Bird. Of course you want love, and so you mean to leave me. I knew the black beast had been at your honey. I forbid nothing. I am also pictured as the most puissant tyrant who ever drew breath, and if I did not garner my energy, I would laugh over this. People will do what they will do, and I do not prevent them. Of course I have my little tantrums, my orders, my imperial ways; doesn't possession of fifty millions of property in this, the great city, allow me some whims? Meanwhile you endure my caresses, poor youngone. I know of course you are planning to run away," and as she said this the Bird moved his head as far as he could to gaze into her eyes. "All the blue skies that ever flew over this sad earth are in that questioning gaze." She kissed him repeatedly on his brow and cheeks. "How many flavors and scents the human face has! As many as there are flowers and grasses! Yet you spurn me. Do I scold you for that? Of course not. Don't I allow both the black eagle and the crone your great-grandfather to love you all they like?

"Having known for nearly a hundred years there is no love under the sickly sun, I have never forbidden it even in those I was getting my best embraces from. I brought you here for many reasons, as you know," she went on, and from her inside pocket she brought out a long gold chain which she put around the boy's neck. He stirred a bit and touched it but showed no other interest in it. "And none of the reasons are what the world would call decent, the employment of you as bait, and so on. Actually all those are factors, but the main factor is simply I wanted you both for yourself and because he wanted you more than any other person living, dead or to be. Yes, you endure my caresses well, my dear. And if you go to Elijah, as I know you are planning to go, you'll have only love. But let me describe his life to you just briefly. Ever since you were born, until today you have known only hygiene, cleanliness, fine victuals, lily-white sheets, entertainment, drives in the park. Of course everybody was indifferent to you, and you, poor darling, singled out by God never to speak, were more at home with birds than men. But when you are translated to the Mime by the black memoirist (who lives under the most imminent sentence of death) you will walk into a world of filth, confusion, exaggerated demands of feeling, a mews of cockroaches, rats, starving pigeons, moths, and spiders who will sting you. But you will go because there is nothing here to stir your mild bird-heart. Therefore not one door will be bolted against your escape with your black lover. Go, and be damned, for I'll never send an arm of the law to bring you back to this perfection of paradise. But be glad, my angel, you can't talk. Your affliction is your happiness. It's talking that has made man lower than the brutes of creation, and is God's most calamitous mistake from which all other mistakes stem. Had the beast never talked, this would be a fairer, greener place, and history, that patched synthetic middling bore of a nightmare, which is eating away even at my brains, would never have been. Thank fortune a thing of such socketless proliferation is fizzling to its finish."

He had fallen asleep at her knees, and without any real difficulty she brought him to her lap, and from a few careless motions of her jeweled fingers his lower clothes, falling, out also fell the globule of his sex, which after an admiring look or two she kissed in way of her present farewell to him, and her recognition of his passing.

Wearing only his beads which descended, it is true, to his kneecaps, intoning his morning prayer to Apollo (he worshipped all the major Greek gods), Elijah Thrush made no sign of recognition of me at all as I stood before him. His eyes looked closed, though they were wide open, and in the illumination of one tiny bulb he appeared indeed, as I remembered somebody's having described him, as if carved out of amber. He came out of his reveries for long enough to point with a curved hand at me, gesturing with it then downward, and I fell on my knees in compliance with his command. I remained a good fifteen minutes whilst he went on with his moaning and sighing, lifting his hands up, letting his head fall down. Prayer has always tired me greatly, and I never knew before how feeble a part of my body I had in my knees, for they pained somewhat fearful.

"Have you taken care of that genetrix of every evil?" he thundered at last, prayers over.

"I have won over the boy to me," I said with some misgiving here.

"Hell-bitch of course knows of our plans," he said as he lifted me up this time from the floor, and I nodded.

"When will you bring the boy here?" he talked now

into his own hands, which were placed like cones over his mouth.

"Whenever you wish, Elijah . . ."

"Oh, can we do it, do you suppose . . . and then, later, once done, where shall we hie to?"

"We can go anywhere," I told him, and hearing this he burst into a flight of laughing notes from the lowest register to a very high one. I remembered then he had also been a singer.

"She just sent me this," he spoke in almost a whisper as he unrolled another yellow telegram, and pushed it into my hand. The message ran:

ALL YOUR PROBLEMS WILL BE SOLVED IF YOU WILL CONSENT TO TAKE MY HAND IN MARRIAGE. BIRD OF HEAVEN AND ANY NUMBER YOUR OTHER MALE SWEETHEARTS WELCOME UNDER OUR ROOF. BUT MARRY WE MUST! THE PERIOD REQUIRES IT. IF YOU REFUSE I HAVE NO CHOICE BUT TO GRIND YOU TO POWDER. RECONSIDER OR PREPARE FOR OBLIVION.

MILLICENT DE FRAYNE.

It was my turn to laugh, but I had only a limited range of notes.

Going into his regular rage, he tore the message out of my hand, walked into his dressing room, and in a trice came out wearing the most elaborate costume I think I have ever seen yet, made entirely of quilts.

"You idiot of a clown, you have an expression on your face out of the silent films," he upbraided me.

"What kind of an answer are you going to give to her message?" I inquired, trying to swallow my own hurt and anger at his words.

"Do you think a person of my degree of eminence

answers such appeals from an old déclassé toff like her?
I wonder the telegraph office does not issue a warrant for
her arrest. Of course the clerks there do not know idiom,
let alone language, and I am sure baboons could transmit
the messages as well as they. For over a half century I
have received a telegram from her nearly every day. The
only time they ceased was a period of forty years ago
when she had erysipelas, though I suspect it was really a
conglomeration of different venereal diseases, for she had
recently been traveling in Madagascar, where she tasted
the semen of a tribe of wild boys living in the mountains.
She came back looking extremely youthful, but paid for
her migration by a ten-year illness. The thing that now
afflicts me, so that I wonder if after all *I* am not running
mad, is simply this: do I require her everlasting obsession
with me, and her cruelty toward me for the sake of feeling I exist? . . . Are you listening to me, Albert? Oh, you
are so distant lately. Now see here. Am I, do you attend
me, am I, Albert, really *her?*"

But the thought of my own predicament suddenly over-
came me with such force, together with a pain in my
head, that I was led to fear I was the party to go insane.
So deadly was the physical pain I put my head on his
shoulder and pressed against him.

"Am I actually Millicent De Frayne, dear Albert?"

"I have seen you together," I told him. "So you must
be separate parties." Then without pause I said, "My dear
Elijah, I am going mad . . ."

"Put aside those thoughts: you're too young for bona
fide madness, and no primitive person such as yourself
can go authentically crazy. Besides, Albert, remember
you are the kidnapper of the Bird of Heaven. Once you
have abducted him tonight, we will both feel better. I
have told you, I think I have, at any rate, that I will take

care of you forever, once you have accomplished the kidnapping. I have recently met a new Maecenas, who promises to supply me with huge sums of money . . . Albert, look at me . . ."

I was awesome ill. I fell at his feet, froth flecked with blood from my tongue and mouth spilling over his naked feet. It was his own "insane" calm which restored me. "You have nothing whatsoever to fear, my good angel," he told me. "I love you devotedly. Not quite with the quintessential love perhaps I feel for the Bird of Heaven, but oh, Albert, so fully . . ."

"A certain creature has total power over me, a winged beautiful thing, my dear Elijah," I tried to tell him the truth. "This is my habit."

"Yes, yes he possesses us all, but you will be saved," he said, showering me with affection, and suddenly my madness did pass. I sat up beside him, and we took a cup of chocolate together.

$\mathcal{S}$tanding before her cream-colored thirteen-foot door, I heard the partially familiar voice of the piano player, Eugene Belamy, addressing Millicent. "Spare me, why can't you. Why must I act against the one I love?"

"Spare *you*," De Frayne replied with such force the door in front of me jiggled furiously. "Tell me, Eugene, have you ever known me to spare myself? Answer me at once, and quit that damnable sniveling!"

"How do I know whether you've ever spared yourself or not, you damned fanfaron!" Eugene retorted. I was so amazed with his spunk, my hand fell from the door-knob.

After a silence I heard him speaking again. "Oh, forgive me, Miss De Frayne, please, please. I spoke so because I'm beside myself."

"As I was saying," she spoke in the chastened reasonable tones of a kind woman wronged, "I'm very hurt you should tell me to my face that you prefer the Mime to me. After all you know where they butter your bread, and it's not at the Arcturus Gardens . . . But to go back to our argument. I am only asking you to betray the Mime for the time being. After you've betrayed him, and he is mine, you will be forgiven by him, you certainly know that, and you'll be restored to your former position. And you're the only one left who can deceive him in the way I require . . ."

"No, no!" Eugene cried.

I heard flesh being slapped again and again and then weeping from Eugene.

"My patience is quite exhausted," she vociferated. I heard a glass tinkle with ice and audible drinking sounds. "Either you betray him according to my method, my dear Eugene," and she stopped a moment to take another swallow, "or I swear I will turn you over to the immigration authorities . . ."

Not having the stomach to hear any more of her browbeating Eugene, I was hurrying away from the door when I heard Millicent cry: "Who's listening there at my door, ho! . . . I say, who's prowling about? Identify yourself there!"

I had become so flustered that I went the wrong way down the hall, and again in my bewilderment, thinking I might by going through the door directly ahead of me come to the exit, walked instead into an immense room I had never seen before, and to my real astonishment saw sitting around a great oak table eight blue-coated policemen, playing cards. They did not so much as look up. In a trice, I went over to where they were sitting, and sat down on a polished stool. My presence scarcely brought a ripple of attention from them, and looking down at myself, I saw that I was indeed dressed formally, like a house servant, but my attention soon strayed from them for I could hear all over again, as distinctly as if it was piped in, the voice of Millicent going on, louder and louder, and Eugene's piteous cries for mercy.

"If you're afraid of Peggs the memoirist, I'm ashamed for you," Millicent's words seemed as close as if her mouth were pressed against my ear, and I could almost feel the current of her breath as I had in past times when I sat at her feet. "When the flag's down, which, since he's black, is all the time, and trouble is his name, and hell his home, he will do anything for you if he thinks you'll ease his torment even for so little as a split second . . . Oh, I know you've fallen for him, that was the risk I ran when I hired a specimen of his superlative, if slightly aging, physical prowess . . . But don't you see, as he betrays Elijah, you betray him. I'm not asking you to use a knife on him—not quite yet anyhow. Kill him another way, where he bleeds the thickest . . ."

At this moment the youngest of the bluecoats, with a set of toothpaste ad teeth, winked at me, and passed me one of his playing cards, which was a matter of fact the five of spades. I put the card in my sock.

"The fuss our people make over our Lord on the cross," Millicent's fierce contralto was on again. "His sufferings after all had a beginning and an end, and in any case had all been prearranged. But consider my case . . ." The same policeman nudged me and passed me another card, this time the two of diamonds, which I slipped into my trousers cuff. "My Golgotha, on the other hand, has

known not only no beginning or end—I am faced at last
with the terror it will continue through recorded time . . ."

I stood up, breathing audibly, but the cop pushed me
down like an usher who will not allow a participant to
leave until the service is at an end.

"And don't forget the Tarbox will kidnap the Bird
tomorrow night, full moon or hurricane . . . And now
for God's sake wipe off your face before you go out of
here, for anybody in the world can tell you've been
bawling."

I was moving now toward the door I had come in by,
without further ceremony, when I heard the bluecoat of
the playing cards say, "Excuse yourself, Albert, when you
leave the room."

And all the policemen around the table began to laugh,
but I caught them off their guard when I began bowing as
low to them as ever black, darky or white had bowed under their detention—for hadn't I observed the Mime's
repertory of pantomime and made it my own as if I had
been his best pupil?

There was a loud round of applause for my performance from the hand of every cop present, and I went on
bowing and pleasing until I had reached the door and
closed it fast behind me.

"Lions! Pelicans! Elephant papers!" I shouted, once I
was safe in servants' quarters, while Norah stared poker-
faced as the seizure came over me.

More than anything else, more than the danger, the
money, the humiliation, the hate of this great house where
I was paid memoirist, it was the language spoken which
was now becoming mine that made me go out of my head.

"I am a peg too low to care what may become of me
now, Norah . . . Bring me wine, hear, a great huge flask
of it, and, hang you, put some motorpower in that white

fat ass of yours. I'll have an ocean to drink before I steal the Bird, or I'll let all eight of those flatfeet plow my guts . . . Cunctator of cunctators!" I screamed at Norah as she raced from the cellar steps with the bottle to uncork it and pour my glass.

"It's all dangerous shoals now, as your mistress would say, Norah, and don't you ever forget 'twas I told you so."

And lying down on the floor, and unbuttoning myself fully, I let the wine slowly trickle over my palate, drop after drop, diminishing it in ceaseless trickle.

My only angel, except one, and my dearest dear," I began my apostrophe to the Bird of Heaven, as he lay sleepless in his trundle bed, his thumb stiffly resting under his nose, his eyes drying slightly from his tears (he cried most of the day, the night). "Are you ready to run over the roof with me to freedom, as you done promised me at our last tryst?"

He nodded dispiritedly.

"Do you still love me and look up to me, orphan?"

He raised his head, and made querulous bird sounds.

I kissed each of his pink toes, and tickled his ribs, but he made no sign of interest or affection.

"So, we will run off together whether you love me or not . . . A warm fur coat, good," I summarized, going over his wardrobe, "fur boots, ahem, and your Scotch highland outfit. Well, you're a pumpkin," I told him, and he grinned a bit then.

Suddenly Millicent's voice rose from a down-the-hall room: "This wine is corked you've served me, you animals! Oh, those rack-brain coves! I'm choking from cork! Yes, you, damn me if I won't beat you the six colors of the rainbow if you don't get your shanks down to that cellar and bring me back a bottle that's had its cork properly removed. Yes, and I'll slap you again, if I want to, for you've no rights after what I've got on you. Down there, on the double, I say!"

"If you don't say you love me, Bird, I vow I won't run off with you," I whispered after the old girl had shut up a bit.

The orphan gave me a finicky kiss on my cheek.

"That's better, Bird." I laced his boots.

"Still afraid the burnt cork will come off on you, I guess," I spoke with the anger coming into my voice. Then the Bird melted me by throwing his arms around me and sobbing. "Shh," I warned, "let her guzzle herself to sleep now, don't raise the alarm . . . That's better, Bird, and now in just a little while we'll be happy, eh?"

"I'm the only one in this place allowed to be on the razzle-dazzle and I'll be blowed if I'll have cork on my tongue again tonight," Millicent's voice came again quite near. I extinguished the bedlamp and the orphan hugged me tight.

"That damned black wagtail is selling his semen again to the help, I suppose," she wailed and then, after pausing lengthily in front of our door, trailed on back to her own sleeping chambers.

"We'll soon be out, and away, and gone." He held on tight to me now just the way you should to your kidnapper. "Over the roofs of the city, you know, to Grandpa's house . . ."

Suddenly the seizure hit me, and I fell to the floor, blood coming out my nose, and trembling, as if I saw the pale horseman. It was him turned on the light, and stared at me. There was no fear in his little rosy face, I mean the blood didn't make him turn a hair. I wiped myself from its major stains, and then putting him on my back, opened the window, and we jumped out on the fire escape and from the fire escape we went to the roof.

There not fifteen paces away were at least three of the eight policemen from the card game.

"Stop or we'll . . ."

Then we heard the bullets, all, all in the unreal way they sound when they're aimed at you, and I felt something sting my elbow, but we were either too quick for them, or we were supposed to get away. We jumped over one building after another, and then down down down to the street and over through soft snowflakes to Tenth Avenue.

I had been nicked in several minor places of my body by the bluecoats' bullets. We couldn't go on to the Mime's until I had inspected myself, and besides in our flight the Bird had lost his shoes, trousers, and his fine fur hat. We were shivering and wet to the bone. We found a deserted warehouse, and hid in the back of it behind some bales of wool, whilst the squad cars went by almost momentarily, the red searchlights came directly into where we were hiding, and the sirens screamed their most maniacal.

I took off all my clothes, but found as I said before only nicks, but once my body was entirely bare, his eyes found out the thing I had kept from the world until then, for when I had given my body before to white people I had always managed to conceal my secret, the fountain of my habit, which I must now tell something of, for my story, my life is coming to an end . . .

My wound, I say, was uncovered, and he put his hand in it, and some matter came out. The Bird showed no revulsion, no nausea, and as I lighted one match after another, the swooning thought came over me that if he would run off with me alone, ditch the Mime, be my all, I could give up my other attachment, if one can call it that.

Taking the word *attachment* and holding his hand I told him the unbelievable, the world of my chambers.

"Have you heard of the *Aquila chrysaëtos*, which is now almost extinct . . ." Then I told him of *this* bird which I had stolen by night from an island, nursed as my own, and one night when he was dying . . .

We looked up into the faces of two policemen . . .

The one immediately took up the Bird, and ran off with him, and the other started to put the handcuffs on me, but my greater strength preventing this, he began to beat me with the cuffs across the mouth.

He let go like he had melted on me when the first cop who had taken out the boy gave out a great yell: "*The kid's skiddooed!*"

I put on my clothes, leisurely, when he had lit out, and then walked to the back of the building. There was the river floating like tar, no moon, snow and rain drifting down, and on the pier far out, yes, there he was all plain as if ten moons shone on him, the Bird of Heaven.

I tried to run, but gave out, and he comes walking toward me, like a sunshiny day in the park, and like we were not runaways or kidnappers.

"Do you want to go away with me, Bird, or go to your great-granddad?"

He half-nodded. "I say, do you want me or the Mime?" I tried him again. Then I knelt down to watch his lips, eyes. "I will take care of you with the last breath in my body. I will make you my habit."

He gave his springtime smile, and took my hand carefully. "But I must tell you what I will give up. I can't go on with *Aquila Chrysaëtos*, Golden Eagle."

He waited, eyes down.

"This fellow until you was the most wonderful thing I had set eyes on, and the only one who trusted me, but he required something more finally than the thousands of dollars daily I had spent on him for imported sustenance, he needed it fresh from the living person, you see, and when all else failed, rather than lose him, I became his living host." I pointed in the direction of my wound. "There was no pain like it, Bird, none under the sun, but there was no pleasure so great either, for it put me with the gods. Yes, I became a spirit because of his high command . . . But if you will go with me, we will leave him . . . Best to kill him, I say, for who'd care for him with their own running blood like me, search the land, you'll never find another Albert Peggs . . . Do you follow my story? I've told it now to the first human being who ever . . ."

"Journeys end in lovers meeting!" a hoarse voice interrupted and brought us up short. We did not even need to turn round to know it was the Mime, who, brandishing a heavy red lantern he had picked up from some street repairman, motioned us to a horse-drawn carriage such as a sightseer might gawk at as it passes in the park.

"We've not one second to lose," he whispered as he gathered us up, and set us beside him in the buggy, and after a few words in Parisian French to the coachman, we went off lickety-split past one waiting squad car after another, each of whose helmeted occupants was oblivious to our passing, and then we headed for the Brooklyn docks.

"Easy, easy, Albert," the Mime soothed me, as I sobbed away in his arms, while I listened to the sound of the horse's hooves on the cobblestones. "Living with that Fifth Avenue felon has caused something to snap inside of you, that's what. Indeed, you may have brain fever, for all I know . . . But as to an eagle touching you, bosh! And so far as his feasting on you, la-la, never . . . But even were this yarn of yours gospel truth, do you think we have time to go to 'chambers' and risk being apprehended by the law! So put your mind to rest about having been the lover of a giant bird of prey, my overwrought precious," he comforted me and took my hand in his. "And please do not presume upon my good nature, but let a slightly older party warn you also against the use of certain *stimulants* in fashion today which I've observed you're no stranger to. Just as wearing to the nerves also is your too generous bestowing of your favors on whoever is paying you the biggest compliments at the moment. Don't let them overstimulate you, I say! You must keep your youth and good looks, as I have, for when they're once gone, you'll have to work by the sweat of your muscles, which, although they more than put the next fellow to shame, won't bring you in the comfortable sums you earn now by being irresistible . . . No, Albert, we shan't go to 'chambers' to have a peek at Cloud Land. That's flat . . ."

I buried my head in his lap and made such an outcry that he began to weaken, and told the coachman to slow down a bit.

"And to think you told all this poppycock to the poor

boy here!" he complained, pushing me away from him now and beginning to stroke his grandson's hair. "What must the lad think, telling him a winged creature feasted on your raw flesh! . . . Well, I see there's nothing to do but turn about and go to 'chambers' to prove at least to the boy here there's no such animal as you imagine, and never was . . ."

"Oh, thank you, Elijah," I said and tried to take his hand in mine.

"You see, as of course you do, it's your winning ways which make me violate my own good sense," he grumbled. "And our delay may cost us everything, and we'll be sent to jail for life . . . Fear nothing," he assured his great-grandson, who looked up now questioning into Elijah's face. "Nothing can harm us. Destiny is for us . . ."

After giving the coachman minute instructions where to go, he went on: "Do you know, Albert, I've pawned everything I own to make our escape tonight: silver, china, old paintings, my rings, and here when freedom is within sight we turn back to the city for the sake of one of your whims, to prove you are the lover of a bird! God, we are all headed for the lunatic asylum. Peggs, you have broken my heart . . . Sometime, in your long life ahead, please learn gratitude if you can . . ."

The carriage stopped.

"Is this it, Albert Peggs?" he roared at me. I nodded. "Very well, all alight now, please, and we'll proceed to take the gilt off the gingerbread . . . I feel like slapping you to sleep . . ."

As there was no elevator service at this hour—indeed, the building was forbidden to tenants after dark, as I have pointed out earlier—we had to walk up four flights of stairs. How my fingers trembled in the dark with my keys. I opened the first door, whilst the boy and the Mime followed close at my heels, then the second larger door, and then at last we stood before the violet-colored little door with stars of silver sprinkled over it. I swore I heard the whirring of his wings.

"Are you awake, my dearest?" I spoke into the cracks of the wood.

"Oh, John-a-Dreams," the Mime muttered. "This beats anything."

"Answer me, for you know I belong to you," I went on, and I began sobbing delicately. "Oh, he's gone, Mime, gone forever. You and Millicent have taken from me my only thing."

"Who in the name of God are you apostrophizing through that sliver of a door? Here with not a minute to lose, the police practically at the gates, ordered to shoot us on sight, and you moon and drool. I won't have it, damn your soul!" and with a sudden push and a shove that testified to real strength he broke open the door, and we were face to face with—nothing.

"There's not even a perch here for your winged creature to have sat on," and surveying the floor, he continued, "Not one dropping. Not a feather. You are a lunatic!" but he had hardly got the word out when we all at one and the same time spied a letter lying on the floor. The Mime picked it up.

"Shall I open the epistle?" he inquired. "It's bound to be from her for she's the greatest anonymous letter writer who ever put quill to paper. It may be an unpleasant surprise for you, Albert, nonetheless . . ."

But I was so overcome by the loss and disappearance of my *Aquila Chrysaëtos*, known to hoi polloi, as Millicent would say, as Golden Eagle, I cared not enough even to go on breathing. But strangely, knowing him to be gone, I felt no return of my usual seizures. I was calm, cool, myself, but now there was like real death in my veins. There was no reason to go on living now he was gone, and as if to prove to the Mime at last that he had once pecked at my vitals, I took off the jewels covering my stomach and exposed the region around my navel, which was one continuous wound.

"Why do you continually expose your person?" he snapped as he looked up from the letter. "Haven't your best parts been praised enough? Don't, pray, be so primitive. Button yourself, and hark to this letter our old whore has written us:

I AM ONLY A FOX'S STEP AWAY DEARS ALL. WHICHEVER WIND OF THE ROAD YOU TAKE 'TWILL BE SURE TO LEAD TO ONE WHO DOES ALL THINGS FOR YOUR OWN GOOD. COMFORT ALBERT ON HIS LOSS, BUT LET HIM TAKE WARNING! HE CANNOT SHARE MY LOVE WITH ANOTHER.

M. DE F."

Then there we were in the carriage again, the Mime victorious for proving me both fool and liar, when gunfire began to sound again from some distant street. "Pay no mind to the rifle shots over there," he advised as he studied my features, "and, indeed, be glad there is street fighting over there, for 'twill draw off the police from pursuing us. Well, Albert, thanks to your morbid imaginings we are late for our boat, but as we are the principal passengers they're duty-bound to wait for us . . . Turn here to the left, why don't you, my good fellow," he called out to the driver now, and as he spoke his spittle flew back and showered me in the face. I reached for the great-grandson's large neckerchief and dried myself off.

"Pray tell what is the meaning now of this delicate gesture?" the Mime said and turned his full attention to me . . .

"I was doused by your sputum, if you must know," I replied sharply.

"In all my years before the public of over four continents, my dear memoirist, I have never been accused of so loathsome a practice . . . Kindly beg my pardon, if you please. I shall insist on it . . ."

I handed back the neckerchief now to the Bird and kissed the latter.

"Albert, I am waiting for an apology."

"None is forthcoming, Elijah," I spoke to him in a shaking calm.

"None whatsoever, my dear?" he spoke sweetly, as he often did when convulsed with rage. "How dare you speak in this fashion to one who has brought you to a true pinnacle of greatness. You would be in the fields cutting cotton this minute had I not rescued you!" he shrieked, forgetting that it was I who had applied to Millicent De Frayne for employment, and that it was she who had introduced me to him. "My besetting sin is I am too generous to my admirers . . . Because I need love so much, I give kindness where kindness is misunderstood, shower blessings where they are taken for common coin, and raise those to glory who would be quite well rewarded with creaking humdrum . . ."

"You don't believe in *him!*" I screamed with such vehemence that a whole mouthful of blood came from my mouth onto his hands and breast.

"Albert, my dear, you have stained me," he said, in a weak but consoling voice. "Albert, my dear, are you quite yourself?"

"You didn't believe in him," I whispered and shook with

sobs, while the Mime taking some old rags out of a pouch which he had at his feet began wiping himself and me free of the blood.

"I believe in him if you believe in him, Albert. I suppose you refer to the eagle," he spoke much as some deposed king might who reads the writ for his own exile. "The docks are right ahead of us. Let us all walk as composedly as possible over the gangplank. Remember the police are not only looking for us, but are prepared to shoot us on sight should we offer resistance. She is behind the whole thing of course, that rouge-caked hag of every human rottenness. Oh, Albert, do you know how I hate her, and how she bores me! And I can think of nobody else! She has expropriated all that was fine in me, dear boy . . . Look at me! Do I not look a ruin. I am not at my best."

He picked up a hand mirror, and smoothed down his hair a bit, and daubed his face with powder.

Then with the slight rigidity and erectness of head and tightness of lip which were characteristic of him just prior to appearing before the footlights, he said, "Shall we prepare to go abroad, gentlemen?"

We heard increased gunfire in close proximity as we were alighting from the buggy, but Elijah appeared entirely to ignore it. But as the shots started coming in increasing frequency, he stopped in his tracks and, putting his mouth close to my ear, confided: "It's as close to a twenty-one-gun salute, Albert, as either you or I may ever come, so for all our sakes, please don't look so downcast!"

As we three went up the gangplank of the ship, thick white flakes of snow fell in even greater quantity, not calculated to give me any feeling of heartsease.

But Elijah all but retraced his steps in the direction of the still-waiting buggy when he caught his first glimpse of the name of our ship, looming out at us in jagged black letters:

QUEEN DICK
FORMERLY
THE PLUCKED PIGEON

An officer in a raincoat as large as a small tent was now advancing toward us, calling out in a barker-like expressionless voice, "Party of Mr. Elijah Thrush—this way, sirs, kindly come forward!"

"But, captain," Elijah's voice boomed loud over the water, "the ship I commissioned was to bear the name *Hors de Combat!*"

And he refused to go another step of the way.

"But it's all one and the same ship, Mr. Thrush," the officer replied, and bringing his feet together he saluted the Mime. Then in a voice which was low enough to be intended only for Elijah he said, "I am not, however, the master of this ship, who is waiting impatiently for you and your party at the captain's table of course . . . Please, this way, sir. You are absolutely on the right vessel, and kindly forget any mixup in names. Can't I carry the youngest chap there? He looks all tuckered out."

"It would be awfully good of you if you would, thank you," the Mime spoke in his higher society manner, "for I don't know of a tot in the whole wide world, unless it be one of the Princes in the Tower, who has suffered lately such vicissitudes as my beloved great-grandson, who is known to us, sir, his intimates, as the Bird of Heaven . . ."

As the Mime prattled on in this fashion, I suddenly turned tail and was running back down the gangplank, when he rushed after me, and pulled me roughly up the plank again, all the while never leaving off his chitchat with the officer, who was carrying the Bird now on his shoulders.

Almost the very next moment we heard the gangplank let down, and the whistles all blew. Yes, we would soon be on the high seas, and here I had no experience with water at all, and would, I was certain, be deathly ill.

We were shown into an ample well-lighted room, and some spirits were brought for Elijah and me, and some hot grapejuice for the Bird of Heaven, who looked like a little corpse floating in the brine.

"No one can know how glad I am to be leaving that impossible city," Elijah was telling me, when another officer, bowing low, came up to us.

"Ah, you are the captain of course," Elijah extended his hand.

"No, I'm sorry to disappoint you, Mr. Thrush, but the captain is, as a matter of fact, awaiting you in the banquet room . . . If you'll come this way, you'll do us a great deal of honor indeed. Mr. Thrush, kindly take my arm, for we must announce ourselves . . ."

"I was booked for the ship *Hors de Combat*," Elijah was saying to the officer, who now that he was leading us to the banquet room seemed not to pay attention to anything more which was said to him, "and as I was explaining to my good friend here, Mr. Albert Peggs, I was quite taken aback by the present name, which . . ."

A great garish orange door opened, and we stood on the threshold of a room which seemed larger than the boat itself. A fancy celebration table for many guests was laid, with candles glowing, great mounds of flowers, such as I had seen only at state funerals, and busy servants were running here, there and everywhere. The air was heavy with the smell of blossoms and roasting meat.

In the center of the table sat a personage wearing a mask. I assumed it to be the captain, although why he wore a mask I would be the last to know.

"My heart finally misgives me," Elijah turned to me, disengaging his arm from that of the officer. "I no longer fear—I *know* we've boarded the wrong ship . . ."

"Your fears, then, were sumptuously in vain, my only angel!" a booming familiar contralto came to us, and off from the "captain's" face fell the silver mask, and there looking out at us were the ancient lineaments of Millicent De Frayne, the world-famous heiress. "You're on the right ship for the first time in your life!" she signaled to Elijah.

Elijah Thrush immediately dashed for the exit door, and attempted to force his way past the restraining officer.

"Manacle him, Belsize," she addressed the aide, "if he makes any further attempt to leave our ship," and the officer ushered Elijah back into Millicent's presence.

I felt the vessel moving now, and fearing I might become seasick, I moved unsteadily over to the banquet table and sat down unbidden some four or five places from Millicent, who was rubbing her hands with her accustomed rose water.

Cupping her hands then, Millicent called out as if to a large gathering in the big room: "This is Elijah's and my wedding banquet!" and with a jerk of her head and a wave of one arm she indicated that the Mime and the Bird of Heaven should be brought to sit beside her. They were more or less carried by four young men whom I recognized at once as among those youths who were always perpetually waiting in her outside hall on Fifth Avenue.

Oh, how unwell I felt, and then suddenly I looked up and what I saw made me so whirling-dizzy I fell like a rag doll to the floor, for in a large glass case, directly above

Millicent, I had caught a glimpse of the stuffed remains of the Golden Eagle, inimitable feathers and all, whom I had cared for and loved for so many months. It could not have been a copy.

"My, what poor sailors we are this evening!" . . . Millicent complained, looking down at me . . . "And I could live on the sea like a cork . . . Hoist up our dark friend, the huskier of you swains, and put him here near my left-hand side, for the banquet's scheduled to begin . . ."

And so there we all were, as if back at Millicent's own Empire apartment, or at an opening night of the Arcturus Gardens.

"Happiness so complete is not without its frightening forebodings, gentlemen all," Millicent began, and then she actually began to weep loudly into a taffeta handkerchief.

"Remember, I have seen the old crocodile at work years before you were born or thought of, Albert," the Mime raised his voice in order to be heard above Millicent's lamentations. "Beware, my boy, for one drop of that distillation of poison from her eyes will burn till . . ."

"Albert, my dear," Millicent interrupted him. "I can never thank you enough for what you have done for me . . . No other memoirist, no other spy, certainly, has been successful in bringing Elijah and me together at last. I have tried, as you know, ever since 1913 to achieve this. You, with your wonderful primitive and yet sophisticated power, have brought this about. As a token of my gratitude to you, Albert, I am giving you your freedom tonight, sending you back as soon as the banquet is over on a private boat, and endowing you for life with a stipend . . . I don't know where Elijah and I will be honeymooning, but we'll drop you a card from port to port . . ."

"Oh, stop her, Albert, and run to the nearest wireless and send an S.O.S. There are still laws in effect in this nation!"

"Ever the country bumpkin at heart, Elijah, believing what you hear on the radio or read in the press . . ."

"I could never go back now, Millicent, and I prefer to stay on shipboard, after all!" I began now to feel some real sense of responsibility toward Elijah's safety and his great-grandson's, especially in view of the fact my Golden Eagle was dead.

But then without warning, a great pain was felt by me in my right ear. It was unendurable, and I held my hand over my earshell.

"Earache often comes as a result of seasickness and/or naughtiness, dearest Albert . . . Pray, let me examine your ear," Millicent leaned close to me. "Ivors fetch me my ear-spoon . . . you'll find it in that old Welsh dresser over yonder. That's a dear . . ."

She took the earspoon from Ivors, one of her retired lovers, and began poking about in my ear. The pain was intolerable, but such a quantity of things began coming out from her ministrations, pieces of cotton, petals of flowers, an insect or two, a gold button, notepaper, that I had to be grateful to her. When she had finished I almost felt myself again, and forgetting Elijah's warnings against her, I kissed her hand again and again until she said sweetly, "That will be about enough, from that bee-stung pair of lips."

"You are both positively disgusting," Elijah cried.

"What's wrong with all and everyone is we're not getting wine!" And she clapped her hands, and several doors opened at once, and more youthful men scantily clad began bringing in bottles and ice.

"To take away all occasion of dissension and superstition," Millicent's voice suddenly took on a kind of priestly cadence, "which any person may have, let me answer him we have the finest bread, as well as liquor, one can procure. The meat will be another story. Eat, and drink, hearties, for you're all the acme of male glory, and it's glory only I live for . . ."

To the considerable astonishment of all, perhaps to Millicent De Frayne herself, the Bird of Heaven of his own volition now seated himself on the aged heiress' lap, and twined his arms about her. She gave him copious drafts of wine.

At this final "reversal of the order of the universe" Elijah broke a lifetime series of resolutions, and took a deep draft of red wine (he had never drunk spirituous liquors or smoked for fear they would tamper with his physical endowment from nature), while Millicent observed him, when not kissing the Bird, with beady-eyed concentration.

"Dearly beloved, all," Millicent began a kind of after-dinner speech, although we were still feasting on the entree, which was some unidentified rather stringy meat, "this is, as you all must know, my wedding day . . . After an engagement of over fifty-odd years, Mr. Thrush and I are to be joined in wedlock on the high seas . . ."

Elijah's hand bearing his most showy sapphire ring shook violently.

"No bridegroom," she went on, "has ever been wooed, pursued, and indeed hunted for so long, without fatigue or loss of interest on the part of the huntress . . ."

At this moment, perhaps feeling extreme weakness and fearing he would lose consciousness, the Mime took a few gobbles of the meat on his solid gold plate.

"What kind of flesh am I eating?" he cried, choking and clasping his throat.

"I have spared no expense, or time, in capturing the only person who ever captured my heart. Mind you, I am not unacquainted with marriage. I have gone through four husbands . . ." She stopped for a moment, like an ancient actress who, come back from retirement, cannot for the moment even recall the one small speech a doting director has assigned her. "Ivors, seraphim, fetch me that little ledger there, nestling on those megaphones . . ."

Ivors also brought her a lorgnette which I had never seen Millicent use before, and which I suppose was reserved for sea voyages.

"Ah, I was mistaken . . . six husbands," she read from the ledger. "But for the love of me, I can't remember the last one's name, and it's not written down here anywhere . . . Ivors, who was he, for I recall we were wed in 1970 . . ."

"Patrick Filkin, madame . . ."

"Oh, no, now you've quite confused me. He was in 1968, forgetful darling . . ."

She consulted a few pieces of loose paper, though getting them in order was a bit of a job owing to her having the added weight of the Bird of Heaven on her lap . . .

"This meat, Millicent, is not quite palatable," the Mime now complained in a more everyday kind of voice.

"Have the steward bring you something less recherché, then, my precious."

She pored again studiously over her notes.

"Good grief, Albert," she put down her lorgnette and looked at me, for I was sitting now some few seats away from her, and had been somewhat occupied, I must confess, with the kisses being bestowed on me by one of the "waiting" young men in Millicent's service. "Albert! These are your own notes, for the good land's sake . . . They're devastating attacks on both of us, Elijah, you should hear what the boy thinks of us!"

"Can you wonder he would write against you, Millicent," Elijah said, helping himself to the escalloped potatoes, "when you've ruined his life." He put down a spoonful of potatoes and looked at me, shaking his head. "You have driven this poor boy from the cottonfields mad, as you've driven everybody who has ever so much as said ten words with you . . . He believes, owing to your unhinging him, that he was a lover of a certain eagle . . ."

"And so he was," Millicent put away the notes she claimed were written by me.

"You ride roughshod over . . ."

But at this moment I let out a great cry, for one of the youths who had crawled under the banquet table was giving me nips with his teeth in very unprotected places of my body.

"Albert had to come out some time, Elijah, and though we were not the right people for him, in this pinchbeck age of ours, the right people might never have come along. I am aware of the hearts I have broken, but it's better to have one's heart broken through those who shower one with attention, than to be ignored, and waste away untouched by the ravages of misdirected feelings . . . Here we are, my dears . . ." she cried, victoriously holding up a legal document. "In 1970 I was married to Honnybun Rolleston."

It was the first time in my life I had ever heard of baked Alaska or tasted it, and Millicent waited for me, not allowing others to touch their plates either, until I had pronounced on it. I said "Yummy grand" again and again as all awaited my judgment.

"I couldn't send the boy away on a night like this without something special on his stomach, could I, Elijah?" she called down the long table to her bridegroom.

"You were never married to Honnybun Rolleston as late as 1970," Elijah flared up and then as if pleased with this statement repeated it again and again.

"You mean my records lie!" She suddenly rose, and as she did so the Bird fell to the floor with a loud bump. An attendant picked the boy up and took him out of the room.

"Sit down, my dear," she spoke tartly to me when I rose in concern over Bird, "and have your steward bring you another helping of the Alaska . . ."

"Lower the lights a bit, Ivors," she intoned, "for the ceremony is about to begin, I daresay . . . Fetch the little casket over there by the bouquet of hyacinths. . . ."

"Oh, verminous old age!" Elijah cried, and I believe that for the first time in his life he was drunk, but since I was being thrown off the ship, I didn't remonstrate with him about his condition and was so confused mentally myself that for the first time in my life I could not remember my own name. I asked Millicent point-blank what my name was, and her eyes narrowed, and I could see this had given her another idea.

At this moment the Bird of Heaven made his re-entry, in a fine new costume, which now I can no longer remember, but I think it was an admiral's suit.

"Now we are all assembled for the ceremony," Millicent said softly.

She began quickly to weep, and clasped her hands.

"In court, Albert, for I suppose you have read the many legends about me, in court I always act as my own attorney, partly to defray expenses, but also because lawyers cannot remember as far back as I. In this holy hour when Elijah and I are to be made one flesh, I will act as my own priest.

Thank you," she said and looked up at what was surely, I realized later, only nothing, but my attempting to see the person to whom she was speaking caused her to laugh.

I now had the giddy feeling I was being present at the marriage of my own parents, and in a loud voice made a request for another tumbler of wine.

"There is no limit to my generosity, Albert," she begun as she studied me, "and though I force myself to many little economies, I never stint where a friend is concerned. As for your eagle, my dear," she whispered in my recently cleaned ear, "forget him, angel, for he would have died in any case. And think how cruel he was to you. All you require now is love, plenty of love, the physical kind needless to say, and you will get all of that you want. Your finest days are ahead, sweetheart . . . As soon as Elijah and I are married, you will please to leave the boat, remember. Thank you for everything, if I don't see you again . . . I've always had to be busier than I wanted to be, Albert, remember . . ."

Music now sounded from somewhere on deck, young men with more flowers came tripping in and placed bouquets on the table, and from some box at her feet Millicent brought out in lightning movements a very unbecoming opal tiara, which she placed a bit askew on her head. The tiara interfered with her use of her lorgnette, and so she had some trouble reading from a little black book.

"Dearly beloved, all," she began.

"I am not listening, Millicent, and I am not in my right mind for you've put something in this wine," Elijah spoke.

"Darling beloved, this is the moment of my highest felicity—come forward all, this is my wedding day . . . With this Ring I thee wed." She picked up an enormous gold ring, and stumbled over to where Elijah sat with head bowed.

"With my body I thee worship, and with all my worldly goods I thee endow."

Having spoken these words, she seized his hand, as one would take hold of an umbrella that gives signs of flying through the worst of an east wind gale, and forced the great ring on his finger, while he let out cries of pain and astonished rage.

"You have done all that need be done, dearest Albert," she turned now to me. "Your career as a memoirist is over . . . Let me assure you of one thing, undoubted angel"—she covered me with kisses—"I not only love you as a woman, but as a mother. I am your mother, indeed. Let no one say that I have not known the joys of motherhood. They lie in their teeth. I have given birth to several children. My servants neglected them, and the poor creatures died, leaving me in wretched spiritual and physical shape. I suffered as a result from caked breast after the birth and death of my fifth child. I know the agonies of lost motherhood . . ."

"You know the agonies of nothing!" Elijah Thrush now rose from his seat, all the while attempting to remove the ring from his hand . . .

"It won't come off, Elijah . . ."

"You, a mother . . . You, anything, but a marmoreal fiend feasting on young men's secrets," he cried. "Release all of us from this prison ship you've arranged . . . I'm going now to the wireless and send through an S.O.S."

As he spoke, he reeled suddenly from all the wine he had drunk, and trying to break his fall, he seized a great vase full of sweet flags, and went down flat on the floor, the flowers scattering themselves over his outstretched form.

"Albert," he cried piteously, "go back to the city, and tell them I have been spirited away. Get help from the authorities. I suddenly feel my correct age, Albert, my child . . ."

I went over to him, helped him up, placed him on a great easy chair, and kissed him goodbye.

"Never say goodbye, my darling, only *au revoir*. There can be no goodbyes between two souls, like ourselves which have known only pain from birth."

I nodded uncertainly.

But before I could say more I felt Millicent's arms about me, and her lips kissing me everywhere. She slipped an envelope into my hand. "Don't look at this until you're safely in the boat, my dear . . . And as the wind is up, ask the steersman for a heavier coat . . . Now kiss the Bird goodbye, for of course he's going with us on our world tour."

I bade farewell to the Bird, who hugged me avidly, and I kissed all the young men who were in waiting to Millicent, and then closed behind me the heavy iron door to the wedding party, and went out on deck to await the arrival of the little motorboat which was to take me back to the city.

The air was very cold indeed, and I accepted a heavy horseblanket of a coat from one of the deck hands.

Disobeying Millicent, as I knew she expected me to, I opened the envelope and saw it was a certified check for just $200,000.00.

I beat on the heavy door in order to express my thanks to Millicent De Frayne but it was as stout and immovable now as a stone wall. Still, despite its thickness, I could hear music inside, and, I thought, the sound of bottles being uncorked.

"You didn't have to send him away!" I thought I heard the Mime's voice. "Why can't I be allowed to have one retainer, when you have a good fifty or more? Don't touch me again!"

"Elijah! Elijah!" I called against the heavy door.

"Your boat is ready, sir," an officer addressed me, and he motioned to a rope ladder down which I was to go. At that moment the music from a band came so forcefully through the door, I would have sworn we were in the wedding banquet room.

"Albert," the officer tugged at my sleeve.

"Just a second, if you please," I listened to the sounds of the melody. It carried me back to a day, a golden day, in my home town, but I could not think of the name of the melody or the happy time in question of my boyhood.

"Do you know the name of that song they are playing?" I inquired of the officer. He cupped his ear, and listened.

"It's an old circus tune," he said, and he kept urging me to come over to the rope ladder.

"It's called 'Red Wing,'" a sailor said, standing near us.

The officer looked reproachfully at the speaker.

"You'll be in good hands now," the officer helped me into the tugboat. "It'll be some good time before you see your friends up there again," he showed a perfect set of toothpaste white teeth, and as one of his eyes did not move at all, I decided it must be glass and that he was a veteran. I could still hear the music and I realized now the song was "Red Wing," but the falling flakes of snow blotted out the thought of Alabama now.

Being from a land-locked part of the world, I understood very little the pilot said to me, and he talked continuously, but as he did not require me to answer, I began to doze a bit, which seemed to satisfy him as much as when I replied to his speeches. There were two or three other naval personnel aboard, but I was the sole passenger.

We had not been out very long when I heard the electric megaphone testing, and then the hoarse Shakespearean voice of Elijah Thrush, coming as clear over the snow and waves as if I were back in the Arcturus Gardens attending a recital or rehearsal.

"My darling Albert, does my voice carry to wherever you are?" he began, and I immediately jumped up and cried, "Yes, it does!"

"Best to seat yourself, sir, for he can't hear you," one of the men in the back of the boat cautioned me. "You'll only make yourself seasick in any case."

"Albert, I miss you more than I can say. I don't know when I've become so attached to a person of your quality and background. You have literally opened a new continent to me . . . But what I have to say, my sweet," and here he cried out in a paroxysm of grief and rage, "the only thing I can say is that I am ruined, irreparably, for all time, the little that's left of me to be ruined. Oh, I will go under the waves, I fear! She's cut me to mincemeat! Of course I don't blame you, and don't blame yourself. Go back to the Arcturus Gardens and take over. Play all my roles, for your physique, if not as marvelous as mine, is certainly something to turn heads for many a weary season to come. But harken well, now, Albert. She's annulling the marriage. She took me into the wedding suite here, and I don't want to be graphic when we're talking over the ocean like this, but she wasn't satisfied with me at all. She's been spoiled of course by a steady diet of perfect men, and a roster of husbands—you remember her not being able to recall them all even with the help of her ledger. Oh, Albert, she's hit me where I have no defense. She's belittled my *membrum virile*, and had the nerve to say that my semen is not of the proper consistency or copiousness. All this in front of the entire company, as she dragged me back to the wedding banquet. She's now in bed with the boatswain, I believe, but she's ruined my public reputation, and hurt my self-esteem. Of course I am not built like a tapir or elephant, but there have never hitherto been any complaints about the size of my sex, never. I am the perfect Grecian model, as all Europe knows. Albert, I will never recover from this slight. She has asked for the wedding ring back. Oh, can you hear me, wonderful faithful boy? It's so unnerving to speak into wild winds and roaring billows and get no answer from you. I know you can't answer for you've no electric megaphone as I have. And our intimate conversation is being shared by hoi polloi of course. There is no privacy any more for choice spirits. And when will I see you again? This wedding cruise may last years. But you must carry on for me, whilst I am away. Assume my name if you like, anything, but keep the Gardens open. They must not close, do you hear, Albert, my heavenly companion. Here I, who don't know starboard from larboard, am taking this long voyage. Aha, the whore has just come back from the wedding room, having worn out the boatswain. Her mode of intercourse is not normal, which should not surprise anyone since the harpy is well over the century mark. I told you, didn't I, how she keeps her youth . . .

"Now, my darling, I must make this clear, for I have no prejudice. Next to the Bird of Heaven, who, by the way, is just wilting away, and won't last the voyage, but I've nursed him all I can, and stood by him, and should he die, we'll have to consign his remains to the waves, though it will kill me of course, but as to prejudice, Albert, you know I have none. I see you as eternally golden, like your poor eagle whom she murdered, and then forced us to eat, as you must have suspected. She claims, Albert, I have condescended to you, and that I, and not she, am an endogamist. I am speaking to you now, Albert, in a special cabin where they've just moved me, though I can see what's going on in the banquet hall. My cabin is named, by the way, "News from the Past," isn't that an example of spite for you. My darling, I never condescended to you, but always shared my heart's secrets with you. 'Twas I forgave you from the first for being her spy and memoirist, and embroiling me in this final kidnapping plot which she has been hatching for a good fifty years. Do I blame you for being the final hand to bring it all about? Never. Not in an ice age. You and I knew and loved one another thousands of years ago. I feel what I am saying is a love letter though spoken over Ocean's dark waves."

At that moment, or thereabouts, a huge display of fireworks came from land, toward which we were rapidly approaching. Some of the display was in letters, but I was so attentive to what Elijah was saying I did not decipher them.

"I cannot appease her, my dear, I who have had countless of satisfied lovers," he was now back on the subject of his prowess. "Not content with denigrating me where I am great, where all the world has poured out its applause and recognition, she has gone on to cast doubt on my origin. She has said my body bears the earmarks of plebeian stock. Can you bear it, Albert—I who trace my ancestors back to William the Conqueror, while as everybody knows she goes back to some Georgia criminals driven out of merry old England by a righteous parliament. If royalty walks the streets of America today, you know where to call, Albert. You come from royal blood too," he went on, after coughing a bit, due, doubtless, to sea air. "My dearest darling, let me say it once and for all, I love you, I recognize your preternatural greatness and sensitivity, you occupy a special chamber in my heart . . . Carry on my work, adieu, she is cutting me off. Why God allows this monster to live . . ."

More circus music sounded, and this time I recognized the melody as "American Patrol," but I was crying so hard, and so seasick, I didn't recall recognizing the tune until several days later when I went over in detail my first experience on the ocean.

A large crowd was waiting for me at the dock. This delegation would have added at one time much to my surprise, but I did not now have enough strength to be surprised.

There in the forefront was Eugene Belamy. "We haven't a minute to lose," he informed me as he embraced me. "The audience has been waiting for over an hour . . . You received instructions, didn't you, you are to fill in for Elijah whilst he is on his wedding cruise . . ."

We drove like the wind through the back streets, empty and black, with their casket-like warehouses, and blue pavement stones. I could not stop crying. I mourned the death of my pet eagle, I mourned Elijah, whom I knew I would never see again.

Then there I was in his dressing room, putting on a few trinkets here and there, and little else. I thought of slipping on his cache-sexe, but—not to belittle him, after what he has suffered—it didn't fit, and stringing myself with beads, and mascara, I walked out on stage to the tiny winking footlights. I saw Mother Macaulay's frightened albeit pleased expression.

"Ladies, and gentlemen," I began, as the piano playing let up for a bit, "I . . . I . . . I," and choked back a sob. "I am . . . Elijah Thrush."